Ruth Ann
and the
Big Green Blowster

Be happy!
Kathy

Ruth Ann
and the
Big Green Blowster

Kathy Luders & Frances Beebe
(Ruth Ann's Daughter)   (Ruth Ann's Mother)

Illustrated by Jeff Jackson

Brown Books Publishing Group
Dallas, Texas

Ruth Ann and the Green Blowster

Manufactured in the United States of America

For information,

please go to

my website:

www.greenblowster.com

ISBN-13: 978-0-615-27645-8

LCCN 2007928906

1 2 3 4 5 6 7 8 9 10

This is dedicated to

My grandmother, Frances Willey Beebe

and

My mother, Ruth Beebe deVally

You know that I have tried my very best. I hope you
are proud of what we have accomplished together and
are smiling down at me from the Highest Country.

With love,

Kathy

P.S. To my Dad . . . thanks for all the rainbows.

Ruth Ann, circa 1925

Table of Contents

Acknowledgments

Once upon a time—almost eighty years ago—*Ruth Ann and the Green Blowster* was begun, and now, finally, it is finished!

Ruth Ann and I have had quite an adventure these past many months, a journey filled with challenge and discovery, surprise and pride, and friendship and support. And though we have come to the end of our story, we have not arrived here alone, for we have been joined all along the way by family and friends.

It is now with gratitude and affection that I acknowledge and thank the following people:

Wade, Ann, and Ryan: If not for your support from beginning to end, I never would have or could have completed *Ruth Ann and the Green Blowster*. But for you, I probably would not have even tried. You inspired me to take the challenge and begin my adventure. Your enthusiasm encouraged me through to its completion. (You even taught me how to use the computer—sort of.) Thank you for keeping me true to the story's origins and for your continued faith in me.

Ray, Patty, Dana, Chris, Beav, and Rossy: I appreciate more than I can say the opportunity I have had to complete *Ruth Ann and the Green Blowster*. Thank you for all of your encouragement and support, but most of all, thank you for letting me run with this and see it through.

Jeff: You have brought to life through illustrations that which I could only imagine. Thank you for not throwing in the towel when I was so difficult about the characters looking just so—especially Ruth Ann. (Now that she is finally done, do you like her—just a little?) Thank you for joining me on this adventure and helping to make this book a reality. I've enjoyed every minute working with you—with the possible exception of time spent at that darned color-copy machine.

Marvin: I learned so much sitting next to you as you worked your computer magic. In particular, I learned that your patience knows no bounds. There never was a "problem" you could not solve, a question (except for spelling) that you could not answer, or a change you did not graciously make. And though I don't know how you did it, you got your computer to do what I wanted before I even knew that I wanted it. How lucky I am that you joined me on my adventure.

Barbara, Marilyn, Marina, Mary Jo, Leslie, Catherine,

Acknowledgments

Linda Kay K., Sarah M., Libby K., Tracy, Janet, Cecilia, Martha, Kathy O., Karen, Terri, Billie Kite, Nancy, Andre, Marti G., Julie, Prema, Dr. Colleen, Michael, Alana, and Pat: You have each in a special way been a part of my adventure. It is because of your support and words of encouragement that I have come this far. I thank you all and shall forever be grateful.

Milli, Kathryn, and the rest at Brown Books Publishing Group: You have provided me with a personal publishing experience and welcomed me to participate in the process, from editing to public relations/marketing. I am not so sure how lucrative this will be, but it sure is educational and fun. Thank you for being so professional and responsive.

Finally, to Rich: Words cannot express how very much it means to me to have had your unconditional support throughout every leg of my adventure. When I only "hoped" that I could, you "knew" that I could. Thank you for making it possible to continue to do it my way.

With love and thanks to you all,

Kathy

P.S. To Will, Emily, Jake, Luke, Evan, and those to follow: This book is really for you. I wish you could have known your Great Gramma Rudy.

An Introduction—of sorts

Only recently have I become acquainted with Frances Willey Beebe. I have come to know her through the pages of her written words. Frances Willey Beebe, my maternal grandmother, died sixteen years before I was born, and yet we have written this book together. Before the music of *The Twilight Zone* begins playing in your mind, let me explain. . . .

When I was just a little girl, about the age that Ruth Ann is in our story, I came across a stack of loose, yellowing, typed pages, rather tattered and unkempt. They were in the bottom drawer of the hall cupboard in the home where I grew up.

I remember asking my mother about the pages and being told they were a story written by her mother for her, when she was about my age.

She did not offer to read her story to me, and I did not ask . . . and so the pages remained where they were. After all, there were other treasures in that drawer far more interesting to a little girl, like Great Grandmother Inglesby's wire-rimmed glasses and Papa's mah-jongg set with all its wonderful tiles and pieces.

Although my mother was a voracious reader and read to me often, as was the case with parents and children in those days, she never did read her story to me. I suppose that I shall never know for sure why we were unable to share Ruth Ann's adventure back then, but I suspect it was just too painful. You see, the real Ruth Ann's mother, my grandmother, became very ill and went off to High Country a few short years after her daughter's fifth birthday.

And so, *Ruth Ann and the Green Blowster*, as it was to become, remained tucked away and seemingly forgotten until some fifty years later, when I once again happened upon the pages in another bottom drawer, the same jagged stack of papers, a little more yellow and a little more tattered with age. You see, Ruth Ann has gone on to join Dukey Daddles on his adventurous journey to High Country, but she left behind a wondrous family treasure.

I read what had been written those many years ago, added to, deleted from, and completed to the best of my abilities, the book as it reads today.

This is how, after all this time, I have been blessed with getting to know my grandmother and have also finally been able to share with my mother her very special story—even if just in my imagination.

Perhaps this is the right time for me to share Ruth Ann's tale with you and all the children, young and old, in need of a little imagination tweaking and a magical ride on the "breath column" of the Green Blowster.

Have fun and be safe out there. You are in for quite a ride—quite a ride, indeed!

Chapter 1

Ruth Ann Is Lonely

"**I** don't care whether today is the day before my birthday or not," said Ruth Ann, gravely. "I'm lonely just the same!"

Ruth Ann was a little girl, very little indeed. She had blue eyes, the color of cornflowers under water, and hair like sunshine on ripe wheat; but she was as little a mite as ever roamed through the spring woods, or ever came to the edge of Cattle Swamp to see whether or not the fireflies were really pixies carrying elfin lanterns. Just to give you some idea of what a tiny, tiny girl she was, I'll tell you this: When she stood very straight and held her head up very proudly, she was only five of her father's hand-lengths from the ground!

It was the day before Ruth Ann's birthday. She had been walking through the woods that stretched behind the great white house where she lived. Her head was bent and she walked slowly.

It was spring and new leaves were sprouting on the trees. Here and there, a lovely wildflower said, "Peek-a-boo! I see you!" from the earth at her feet.

Still, Ruth Ann was lonely. You see it was this way. . . .

Dukey Daddles had gone away forever. Dukey Daddles was Ruth Ann's dog. He was half police dog and half Airedale. He had lop-ears and curly-haired skin. He had chased sticks and brought them straight back to Ruth Ann. More importantly, Dukey had understood every word that she had said when the two of them had taken their walks through the forest to the edge of Cattle Swamp.

But a very sad thing had happened!

The house where Ruth Ann lived was set on a boulevard where great trucks passed, taking vegetables into the city from country gardens. Dukey Daddles had run across the street in front of a truck but had not been quick enough.

Even though Mother had tried to comfort her daughter by assuring her that Dukey Daddles had gone on to a truly delightful place up high in the sky, Ruth Ann was still very sad and lonely.

"It's simply terrible," she remarked to herself. "Of course, I love Mother and Daddy, but Dukey Daddles was a *friend*. A friend is different somehow!"

The young girl was now approaching her favorite resting place in the woods, a small hillock that she called Giant's Cap.

It was shaped exactly like a cap and was just the right size for a giant, if indeed giants wore caps. Ruth Ann wasn't so sure about that!

She and Dukey Daddles used to walk to Giant's Cap almost every afternoon. They sat on the small mound and thought of the most remarkable things. They saw the most remarkable things, too!

Once a tiny field mouse had run out from his house and taken off his little feathered hat to Ruth Ann and said, "Good afternoon!" very politely. When Dukey Daddles had barked back, "Good afternoon," the mouse had become frightened and had run away. He had not understood dog language.

Sometimes, Ruth Ann and Dukey would sit for awhile and watch the Smilies as the spritely woodland fairies went about their business in the trees, coloring the leaves of the woods in the fall, or helping some of the baby buds to get out into the air at the beginning of springtime.

It had been such a wonderful world when Dukey had been alive to share it! Ruth Ann gave a sigh that came clear up from her toes, and she stumbled a bit because her eyes had filled with tears, and she could not quite see where she was going.

That very instant, the most surprising thing happened!

Chapter 2

A Strange Acquaintance

ave a care!" came a cracked little voice from the ground at her feet. "Have a care! It's been such a dry winter that if you step on me with one of those big feet of yours, I'm done for!"

"Goodness gracious!" exclaimed Ruth Ann, stepping back and looking down at her feet in utter amazement. "Where are you, and *what* are you?"

"Why, I'm right here before your eyes," came the cracked voice, crossly this time. "One more step and you would have written 'finished' after the story of my life!"

"Oh," cried Ruth Ann, "I see you now!" And she stooped down closer to inspect an odd little man at her feet.

He looked like a tiny stick with twigs sticking out of his body for his arms and legs. His head was like a knob at the end of a stick, and his mouth was a wide crack in the wood. Just now his eyes were shining with fear and his nostrils quivering with excitement.

"Why do you lie so still when someone is going to step on you?" asked Ruth Ann. "Can't you get up and run out of the way?"

"No," explained the wooden man, grumpily. "I can't move my outside joints at all any time, and this is the worst possible season for my insides. I'm still cold from the winter frost, and my sap hasn't begun to flow well yet."

"I see," Ruth Ann nodded. "Then you're not connected with a tree or anything, are you?"

"No," answered the gruff fellow. "I'm all alone in the world now, but I used to be a whistle and belong to a boy!"

"A whistle!" cried Ruth Ann delightedly, and she took the stick up in her hands to examine him more closely. "Then I shall call you Whistle Stick! It suits you exactly."

"Eh, one name is as good as another, I suppose," grumbled the stick. "When the boy and I were together, we had a glorious time whistling the merriest tunes! But two years ago I fell out of his pocket while we were walking through these woods, and since that time I haven't been able to make anyone take any notice of me. It isn't pleasant to be alone all the time. And that's for sure!"

"Whistle Stick, I'm so sorry for you," said

Ruth Ann. "I know exactly how you feel. Just the other day my very best friend, Dukey Daddles, was run into heaven by a truck."

"That's so?" remarked the stick. "Who was this Dukey Daddles?"

"He was my dog," she explained, "and I loved him more than anything else in the whole wide world. I'd give anything to see him again!"

"Humph!" grunted Whistle Stick. "Dogs like to chew wood too much to suit me, but to each his own taste. However, I'm glad you happened along just when you did, for I need someone to help me with an experiment."

"An 'experiment'?" Ruth Ann was puzzled. "That's a big word, 'experiment.' What does it mean?"

"It means," explained Whistle Stick, "that I have something that I would like to try, and I need you to help me. Will you?"

"Indeed, I'll be glad to help you in any way that I can," replied Ruth Ann, politely.

"Well, now," continued Whistle Stick, "do you see that hole in the maple tree standing two bushes to the right of here?"

Ruth Ann looked and nodded her head.

"Two evenings ago," he went on, his voice sinking to a husky whisper, "two evenings ago, the Smilies were working on the baby sprouts. When they got through, they put their acorns full of growing grease into the hole in that old maple tree. Now, more than anything else, I'd like to be able to move and walk about like a child. I have an idea that if you could get the grease from the acorn pails and rub it on my stiff joints, I could walk and move my arms and legs whenever I wanted to, just the way you do!"

"What a perfectly splendid experiment!" shouted Ruth Ann, clapping her hands. "I'll see right away whether I can find the acorns or not!"

"Wait a minute! Wait a minute!" ordered the stick gruffly. "You can't do anything like that in broad daylight, you know! You'll have to wait until midnight."

Ruth Ann's excitement quickly turned to disappointment! "I'm afraid that I won't be able to help you, after all." She sighed. "My parents never allow me out alone after dark. Besides, this is the night before my birthday, and I certainly don't want to do anything that will upset them."

"Shucks and nonsense!" exclaimed Whistle Stick. "They wouldn't mind if you came out here tonight to do me a good turn. Of course, if you came to the woods at night just because you wanted to be naughty and disobedient, that would be an entirely different matter. But when you are coming to put growing grease on an old stiff like me, to make a new man of me, your errand is one of unselfish service, and I'm sure your parents would want you do something kind like that!"

"Well," mused Ruth Ann, "it does sound different somehow, when you put it that way. I guess I'll try it!"

"Now you're talking," cried Whistle Stick, with the first real pleasure he had shown. "I'll expect you then about midnight. That's the only time for an adventure like ours!"

"How shall I know when midnight comes?" asked Ruth Ann. "I'm a very sound sleeper."

"I'm glad to hear that," said the stick. "It proves that you are a good girl and have nothing to dream bad dreams about. I'll tell you how you can wake at midnight. Pay close attention, please!"

Ruth Ann leaned forward obediently.

"Tonight after you've put on your pajamas," explained the little man, "and before you go to sleep, stand at your window with your hands outstretched to the east. Then say three times very softly:

Moon clear,

Moon dear,

Full moon over the maple trees,

Shine white,

Shine bright,

Open my eyes at midnight, please!

"You'll find out," finished Whistle Stick, "that exactly at midnight, your eyes will pop open. Then you can creep quietly out of the house and run here to me!"

"Oh," breathed Ruth Ann, happily, "doesn't it sound wondrous! Are you sure that I'll wake up?"

"That charm never fails," Whistle Stick assured her. "I'll be waiting for you."

"Then I'd better go right home to supper now," cried Ruth Ann, "and get to bed early so that I'll be all ready for our Great Adventure."

Softly and with care, she set the stiff little man down on the ground at her feet. Then waving goodbye excitedly, she turned and ran back through the woods to the great white house on the hill.

Chapter 3

Concerning Growing Grease

hat's the matter with Ruth Ann?" asked Father.

It was an hour later, and Mother had helped Ruth Ann with her bath after she had come in from her walk through the woods. The three of them were now at dinner.

In front of Ruth Ann was a huge bowl of hearty stew, and beside her plate was her own special cup of rich milk. There was a piece of gingerbread too, as light and delicious as Mother could make it.

Father was worried.

"What's the matter with Ruth Ann?" he repeated. "Her cheeks are flushed and she's barely touching her food!"

"What's the matter, Ruth Ann?" Father asked her directly this time.

"Why . . . why nothing, Daddy," she stammered. She didn't know what to say. The adventure that she and Whistle Stick had planned for midnight was really the little man's secret and not hers. She didn't dare tell her father, and yet she hated to keep anything from him, so she just cast her eyes down at her plate and began to eat her stew.

"Has the child a fever?" Father asked, looking again at Mother.

"No, dear. Perhaps her cheeks are flushed from her bath."

Ruth Ann gulped down the last bite of gingerbread and drained the last drop of milk.

"I . . . I guess I'll go to bed," she informed her parents.

"Now I know the child is sick!" exclaimed Father. "That's the first time in her life that she has ever wanted to go to bed at the proper hour!"

Mother just laughed.

"Most probably it's excitement over her birthday, dear," she told Father. "Don't you remember how thrilled we used to be over our birthdays when we were Ruth Ann's age?"

Father seemed to remember, for he grinned at Mother and said no more.

Mother took her little one upstairs and helped her into a clean pair of pink pajamas.

After listening to Ruth Ann's prayers and tucking her snugly in bed, Mother turned out the light and tiptoed out of the room as though Ruth Ann were already asleep.

In truth, Ruth Ann was not asleep—far from it! She lay listening to Mother's footsteps as they crept down the stairs. When they had grown very faint, Ruth Ann jumped out of her bed, ran to the east window, and stretched her arms out exactly as Whistle Stick had told her.

Moon clear,

Moon dear,

Full moon over the maple trees,

Shine white,

Shine bright,

Open my eyes at midnight, please!

She repeated the words of the mysterious charm two more times very softly and then crept back to bed, covering herself clear up to her eyes. She felt very daring and very excited. She did not expect that she could ever fall asleep; but the room was filled with the loveliest gray shadows that grew closer and closer, until she felt warm and snuggly under the cozy quilt Grandmother had made especially for her. Very soon, Ruth Ann's eyes closed and she was fast asleep.

It seemed no time at all until she woke with a start. It was as if someone had put light fingers on her eyelids. She sat bolt upright in bed. Confused, she rubbed her eyes and looked about her. The lovely gray shadows had run back to the far corners of the room, and peeping over the window sill was the most wonderful full moon! The light from it covered Ruth Ann's pillow and it was the touch of the moonbeams that had felt like someone's fingers on her sleeping eyes!

Instantly it all came back to her—Whistle Stick and their Great Adventure! She jumped out of bed in a jiffy.

"The charm worked! The charm worked!" she whispered happily to herself. "Now for the woods!"

She did not even wait to change into her play clothes, although she did take time to slip into her shoes, for the path to the woods was pebbly and full of briars. Creeping very softly, so as not to wake Father and Mother, who were asleep in the next room, she crossed to her bedroom door, opened it so gently that not one squeak could pierce the heavy silence, and began to descend the stairs.

Once down the steps and across the hall, the rest was easy! A click of the night latch on the huge front door, and she was out in the bewildering moonlit world.

"How different the world is under the moon," she thought. "It's prettier somehow, and yet makes me feel sort of trembly in my stomach. I do believe I'm just a little afraid!"

Ghostly shadows played about her everywhere. The maples waved mysterious arms at her as the night breezes moved through their silver branches. Tall lilac shrubs looked like witches in long gray cloaks. Stately hollyhocks bent toward her, nodding elfishly. Small gurgling laughter came from low sweet berry bushes on the front lawn!

Ruth Ann ran swiftly around to the side of the house and across the field to the woods. There, the great maples and oaks with their shadows doubled the mystery and the thrill. She could not hesitate, for she must help poor old Whistle Stick! She had promised to do all that she could to help him move like a child.

Quickly, she made her way in and out among the ghostly trees with their low-hung branches. At last she sighted Giant's Cap, and soon after, the familiar squeaky voice assailed her from the ground at her feet.

"Well," he said crossly, "I'd almost given up on you."

"Whistle Stick," panted Ruth Ann, taking him tenderly into the shelter of her warm hand, "I'm sorry if I am late, but . . . isn't the woods a spooky place in the middle of the night?"

"What if it is! What's the matter with spooks? Most of them are nothing but kind old men in gray beards . . . and I like 'em!"

"Ooh," shuddered the little girl, "have you really seen them?"

"Plenty of 'em. Plenty of 'em!" Whistle Stick dismissed the subject carelessly. "But let's not talk about spooks. Let's get to work on *me*! What about it? Do you still think you can get me the Smilies' growing grease?"

"I told you that I'd do the best I could for you," said Ruth Ann, bravely.

"Suppose you begin then," ordered the little man in his gruffest of voices.

Carefully Ruth Ann approached the big maple two bushes to the right and looked into the hole in the tree that was just about as high as her shoulders. What she saw inside made her cry right out loud with delight!

"Look! Look! There are the acorn buckets sitting on a little shelf. Oh, what beautiful stuff the growing grease is!"

Inside of the little acorn pails glimmered the loveliest liquid that Ruth Ann had ever seen! It was like melted opals. It had the blue of the deep sea in it, and silver like a spider's web, and the pink of the sunset clouds, with a touch of green from a parrot's feather!

"Bring it out! Bring it out!" commanded Whistle Stick, impatiently. "We'll see whether or not it'll fix me up. Besides, I never say anything is beautiful—unless it works!"

"I just know that this can do anything in the world," replied Ruth Ann. "Isn't it the most glorious stuff?"

Very tenderly she lifted two of the tiny acorn buckets with their precious oil from the shelf in the old maple. She held them out so that Whistle Stick could see them.

"Humph! Not bad, at that!" he grunted. Even he was taken by the marvelous beauty of the growing grease.

"Now, if you'll tell me how and where to rub it on you, we'll see whether or not it will help you to move your joints."

"Just rub it on with your finger. I think you'd better try it on my neck first. That seems to be the stiffest part of me."

Ruth Ann took some of the glorious stuff with her finger and rubbed it softly, but swiftly, over old Whistle Stick's motionless neck.

"Try moving your neck now," she whispered, excitedly. "I've gotten the growing grease all over it."

Very slowly, very laboriously, the stick brought his head forward and then moved it back. It was stiff from long disuse and it squeaked terribly.

"Oh," groaned the old fellow. "Please put a wee bit more on. I squeak so that I can't hear myself think!"

She put a bit more of the grease on Whistle Stick's neck. Soon he moved it faster and faster, forward and back, and side to side, until it was quite limber!

Joint by joint, Ruth Ann greased her newfound friend until, at last, he stood upright on her hand and stretched his arms over his head in sheer delight!

"I've come alive!" he shouted. "I've come alive! Isn't motion the most wonderful thing?"

"Yes, but . . . ," said Ruth Ann gravely, for she had been thinking as she watched the little man move about on her hand, ". . . but you're really dangerously small! Why, even when you stand upright, no one in the world will notice you. I wonder . . ."

"Well, now what do you wonder?" said Whistle Stick, rather brusquely, for he was a bit taken aback by this new difficulty.

"I wonder," she mused, more than half to herself, "what would happen if I put some of the growing grease on the very top of your head?"

"Don't try it! Don't even think it!" he exclaimed, alarmed. "I'd look handsome, wouldn't I, if my head grew three times its present size and the rest of me kept right on being small! No! No! Ruth Ann, we've experimented enough for one night. I can move and that's really what I wished for most. Let's just let it go at that!"

"But, Whistle Stick," urged Ruth Ann, disappointed, "I wanted you to be my friend now that Dukey Daddles is gone, and you can't be my friend when you are only three inches

high! Why you're no bigger than Thumbelina! You could curl up and sleep in a walnut shell!"

"Well, have it your own way," grumbled Whistle Stick, after a moment's pause. "But if I turn out some silly looking thing that you're ashamed to be seen with, remember that I warned you!"

Ruth Ann interrupted him with excitement.

"Wait! I have a better idea," she cried. "I'll put the growing grease on the tips of your fingers and on the tips of your toes, as well as on the top of your head. Then you ought to grow evenly all over!"

"All right, all right." He still seemed uncertain about the result of this new undertaking. "But remember, I'm taking on none of the responsibility. Understand that!"

Not to be discouraged, Ruth Ann fearlessly began to rub the growing grease on the little man's head and fingertips and on his toes. Whistle Stick, however, watched her operations with grave doubt on his face.

It took only a moment for Ruth Ann to see that her experiment was a success and to cry out in delight. Very soon, however, she was obliged to set him on the ground! His arms were lengthening and his legs were stretching longer. His head and body were growing straight up into the air!

She kept on rubbing in the growing grease until he stood only about an inch shorter than Ruth Ann herself, and she could look straight into his eyes!

"How perfectly splendid!" she cried. "Why you couldn't be a better size for a friend if you had been made to order."

"Don't I look a bit too thin?" asked Whistle Stick, who had been looking himself over carefully and comparing himself to Ruth Ann.

"Well, you don't seem to have grown out sideways much," she replied, truthfully. "Still, I think you are just right for a Whistle Stick. If you were a boy, that might be different."

"At any rate, that was a good idea of mine to put growing grease on my head so that I could grow tall," said the stick, with pride.

"Why, Whistle Stick, that wasn't your idea!" began Ruth Ann. But then she stopped abruptly, for he was preening himself like a peacock, and he was so pleased with his new appearance that Ruth Ann just couldn't say anything to hurt him! She quietly caught up the acorn buckets with their precious oils and carried them back to their shelf in the old maple.

"There," she exclaimed, as she rejoined Whistle Stick. "That's over. Now what shall we do?"

"What is there to do?" His voice seemed to have grown in volume and gruffness with the man himself.

"We might take a walk," suggested Ruth Ann. "Dukey Daddles and I used to love to take walks, though we never did walk in the moonlight."

"That's a fair idea," grunted Whistle Stick. "Perhaps a walk will limber my joints up more, although they seem to be moving quite acceptably. I don't suppose you've the least idea how wonderful it is to be able to feel yourself move for the first time! That's the big disadvantage of being a human from babyhood. When you moved for the first time, you were too young to appreciate it; but I lay perfectly still for so long a while that I know what a relief it is to be able to bend and move about when you feel like it! Now, come on. Let's go, if we're going!"

Just as Whistle Stick ceased speaking, there came the strangest sound from the direction of Cattle Swamp. It sounded like a mighty puff of wind, like a huge frog's croak, and like a giant cow's moo—all at once. It made little shivers chase one another up and down Ruth Ann's spine.

"What is that terrible noise?" she asked. Her voice was trembling; she was so frightened.

Whistle Stick appeared rather unconcerned when he answered, "I've heard the night people say that it's the breathing of a monster called the Green Blowster. I've heard it often as I have lain here on the ground. Shall we walk there and have a look at it?"

Chapter 4

Introducing
the Green Blowster

hadows deepened in the woods. The moon was much smaller now and shone from a height far overhead.

Ruth Ann, although she had grave doubts as to the wisdom of her course, conquered her fears and slipped her arm through that of Whistle Stick. The new friends set out walking silently in the direction of Cattle Swamp.

As they drew near to the swampy land, the terrible breathing of the Blowster grew louder and louder. Ruth Ann could not help but shudder.

"Oooh." She shivered. "Aren't you frightened?"

"No," replied Whistle Stick, with his customary gruffness. "I can't say that I am. Perhaps I haven't been alive long enough to be afraid."

"Well, I am," confessed the little girl, "and I am getting more and more frightened every moment!"

"Why are you scared?" inquired Whistle Stick.

"What if the Green Blowster got angry and killed us?"

"As far as I am concerned, I'd consider it quite an honor. It isn't everyone who has a chance to be killed by such a terrible monster as the Green Blowster!"

"There's some truth to that," admitted Ruth Ann, encouraged by her friend's remark.

The two had been talking in whispers because loud tones seemed out of place in the dark hours of the night. By this time they had come to the very edge of the swamp. The ground was very muddy and under the moonlight showed the hoof marks of hundreds of cattle that belonged to Ruth Ann's

father. Cattle Swamp itself was about three acres in size. It was covered with lush grasses and cattails. In the very center of it was a large pool made by a spring that bubbled up from the middle of Earth.

Ruth Ann and Whistle Stick stood at the edge of the swamp and tried to determine from just where the Green Blowster's breath was coming.

"There's no doubt in my mind," said Whistle Stick. "I believe that the monster is over there, on the pool."

"It does seem as though the breathing is coming from that direction," agreed Ruth Ann. "How are we going to cross all this swampy ground?"

"Walk across!" grunted Whistle Stick. "Good clean mud never hurt anybody. Take off your shoes and leave them here on the edge of the swamp until we come back, if you like."

"What if we never come back?" she whispered, still a bit uneasy about meeting the Blowster face to face.

"In that case," assured Whistle Stick, "there's no need at all to worry about getting muddy, because we'll never return to be scolded for it!"

In spite of Stick's assurance, Ruth Ann took off her shoes and put them very carefully at the edge of the swamp on a piece of dry ground higher than the rest.

"Ready?" asked Whistle Stick.

"Ready!"

Picking their way through the muddy ground, so as to avoid the puddles and also any snakes that might be drinking there in the still dark hours of the night, the two friends slowly drew near to the pool.

The breathing of the Green Blowster grew more and more terrifying as they crept on. They were so close to the thing now that they could even make out its outline. It sat squat in the middle of the pool like some huge frog!

"Isn't it *enormous*!" Ruth Ann whispered. "It could swallow us as easy . . . as easy as a frog could swallow two flies! I do hope it isn't having a spell of temper!"

"Its breathing sounds about as usual," declared Whistle Stick, after a pause during which he inclined his head to listen carefully to the Blowster's breath. "Let's get around to the front of it where we can see just what it looks like. The moon tonight is nearly as bright as the sun."

The two friends stole around the dreadful creature until they stood directly facing it from across the pool. There they placed themselves behind a clump of cattails and from that

vantage point peered out at the Blowster. It was truly a terrible sight!

It looked more than ever like a giant frog! Its eyes were huge and red like blood, and a great tongue lolled out of one side of its mouth, in the manner of a Pekinese Poodle. Every moment a great breath from its internal cavern would pour from its mouth and nostrils. Each breath was accompanied by the sound that was like a mighty puff of wind, and like a huge frog's croak, and like a giant cow's moo—all at once!

As the two watched the dreadful thing, it yawned! Its enormous mouth opened, and it seemed to Ruth Ann that she could see for a mile down the frightful creature's throat! Its open mouth was so huge that the top lip was lifted almost to the sky and its lower lip had sunk to the bottom of the pool!

The sight was too much for Ruth Ann. She screamed!

"Now you've done it," gasped Whistle Stick, who was evidently *not* so unafraid of the Blowster as he had made out.

He grabbed Ruth Ann's arm and tried to pull her still farther behind their screen of cattails, but he was too late. The huge mouth of the Green Blowster, that had opened so wide for the yawn, shut tight with a clack as loud as the shot of a cannon.

"Who dares come to the retreat of the Green Blowster in the most holy hour of the night?" bellowed the Blowster as its great voice thundered over the pool and Cattle Swamp.

Ruth Ann shook from head to foot; the Blowster sounded so bloodthirsty!

"Answer me," demanded the Blowster, "or I shall blow the skin from off your bones! Who goes there?"

Realizing that an attempt to get away from the huge creature was now worse than useless, Ruth Ann crept out from behind her shelter of cattails.

"It's . . . it's only me, Mr. Blowster," she stammered.

"You'll have to speak louder," roared the great frog-like creature. "There's one thing with which I have no patience, and that is when something is the matter with one's breathing. Take a deep breath and try again!"

"It's me . . . it's Ruth Ann!" This time she positively yelled across the short space to the monster.

"That's some better, but not right yet," he thundered back. "What's that funny looking thing with you?"

"That's my very good friend, Whistle Stick!" yelled Ruth Ann, patting the Stick on one shoulder so that he would not feel bad about the way that the Blowster had described him. Above all things, she wanted to have no trouble with this great creature of the swamp!

"My eyes are not so good as my breath," came the Blowster's bellow. "You'll have to come over here closer where I can see you."

"How will we get there?" asked Ruth Ann.

"How do you get anywhere?" answered the Green Blowster.

"Walk!" shouted Ruth Ann.

"Well then, walk!" yelled the monster.

"Walk? On the water? We can't walk on the water; we'll drown!"

"What makes you think so?" bellowed the Blowster. "Ever try it?"

"Yes. I sank in!"

"That's because you didn't have me to help you do it properly. Does your friend breathe?"

"No," answered Whistle Stick for himself. "I never bother to draw a breath."

"Well," huffed the Blowster, "you don't know what you are missing! Now, if you'll pay close attention," he said, turning his huge eyes toward Ruth Ann, "I'll direct you exactly how to walk here to me."

"But what about Whistle Stick?" Ruth Ann was alarmed at the thought of a closer encounter with this hideous creature. "May he come, too?"

"If he likes," thundered the Blowster, "but if he doesn't breathe, he's lighter than water and can walk over here without any directions from me. Now, I'll tell *you* how to get here: Take in a few deep breaths, but don't blow any of them out. Don't be afraid if you feel yourself swelling, because you won't burst. Then start out across the water, and you'll find that the air in you will hold you up. Are you ready?"

Ruth Ann stood as straight as she could and drew in several breaths that went down to the very tips of her toes. She did not let any of them out. Slowly she felt herself inflating like a circus balloon. Her feet began to rise and she shrieked to Whistle Stick:

"Hold me down! Hold me down! I can't keep my feet on the ground!"

"You had better breathe out a little of that air," cautioned the Blowster, in his thundering tones. "You're too wobbly."

"That's better," declared Ruth Ann after she had followed his advice and let out a few breaths.

"You needn't hold me now," she said, turning to Whistle Stick. "Let's see if we can make it."

Grasping tightly to Stick's hand, she set out across the water. To her amazement, she floated, rather than walked, skimming the surface of the pool as lightly as Whistle Stick himself! They paused immediately in front of the Green Blowster, who grunted his approval in a breath so like a whirlwind that it lifted Ruth Ann and her friend right off their feet for an instant.

"You follow orders very well, indeed," praised the enormous creature. "Exhale please, and then find seats on any of the water lily pads!"

After Ruth Ann had let out all her breaths, she and Whistle Stick looked down and found that they were surrounded by a great mass of water lily pads, as huge for lily pads as the Blowster was for a frog. They found a thick one with a mound in the center, where its stem ran off into the depths of the water, and seated themselves on the hump.

"Now, if you're comfortable," said the Blowster, "we can have a quiet talk. After I find out more about you, I'll be able to decide just what to do with the both of you."

Chapter 5

The Breath Column

 n the first place," began the Green Blowster, after the two friends had seated themselves comfortably, "what's your *line*?" He was looking directly at Ruth Ann as he spoke.

"My . . . my *what*?" The strange question confused her.

"I mean," explained the Blowster, "just what is it that you do? What you work at and try to do very well is what your *line* is. A teacher's *line* is teaching, and a dancer's *line* is dancing, and a builder's *line* is building. It's always the first question that I ask when I am trying to decide whether to swallow someone up or just blow them away forever. You know, it is very important to try your best to do something worthwhile."

Ruth Ann thought this over for a minute.

"But you see, Mr. Blowster," she admitted finally, "I'm not really very big. You don't expect much from very little girls, do you?"

"I expect them to have at least an idea of something that they can do," stated the Blowster, "although I must confess that I do not know much about little girls. How about you?" The creature turned abruptly to Whistle Stick. "Have you got a *line*?"

Whistle Stick was finding the question as difficult to answer as Ruth Ann had.

"I used to make quite merry little tunes when I was the boy's whistle," he stated finally.

"That doesn't count at all, not at all," declared the Blowster. "Your *line* has to be something that you do all by yourself. You couldn't have made a sound if the boy hadn't lent you his breath."

"I guess that's so," admitted Whistle Stick, hanging his head. "You see I'm in the same trouble as Ruth Ann. I've only been able to move by myself for a short while. I wasn't really *born* until Ruth Ann rubbed growing grease on my joints a little while ago."

"Well, if you aren't the strangest pair I ever blew up against!" exclaimed the Blowster, scratching one ear reflectively. "I declare I don't know whether it's worthwhile letting you go on living here or not. Now in my own case, my *line* is breathing. I've known just what I could do best from the time I was a tadpole!"

"Then you *are* a frog!" burst out Ruth Ann. "I just knew it!"

"I am NOT a frog," corrected the monster, severely. "I AM THE GREEN BLOWSTER, the greatest breather in the whole world!"

"Oh, I do beg your pardon," said Ruth Ann, quite humbly.

"As I was saying," continued the great creature, mollified by the apology, "when I was nothing but a tadpole, I knew what I wanted to do best. I determined to be the greatest Blowster in the world. I took breathing exercises most of the day: inhale, 2, 3, 4; hold, 2, 3, 4; exhale, 2, 3, 4. You know how they go. I understand they do something of the sort in classes now, a very good practice indeed . . . but to continue with my story. I breathed so much and so well that my lungs kept growing larger and larger until they pushed my skin out. Thus, I grew bigger day by day. At last my family, the frogs, circulated a petition," here the Blowster's voice assumed a very sad and dejected tone, "circulated a petition, mind you, to have me removed. They claimed that I was a menace to the community, and that the rest of the creatures of the pool were not safe unless I was put away where I couldn't harm any of them!"

"That's terrible!" said Ruth Ann, "And after you had worked so hard on your breathing, too!"

"I've always heard that a great artist has a lot of trouble to contend with," added Whistle Stick, wisely.

At their expression of sympathy, a kindlier gleam crept into the eyes of the monster.

"I can see that there's hope for you both to pick out quite acceptable *lines*," he commented approvingly. "You have already acquired an ability to recognize a great being when you see one.

"However, my life hasn't been such a hard one. Of course, after that petition, I was forced to sink to the beginning of the springs, way down in the bowels of Earth. I am only allowed to come up here on top for a few hours every night. Those hours repay me for all my trouble, for it is then that I rule like a king! Now, listen!"

The monster settled himself down and drew in a great sucking breath. The force of his inhaling dragged leaves and small reeds past Ruth Ann and Whistle Stick as if they had been minute atoms caught in a whirlwind. Insects of the night, caught in the great breath, spun round and round and finally vanished in the Blowster's jaws. As the breath entered his body, the creature swelled almost twice his normal size, and then, as he expelled the air, there came that sound that was like a mighty gust of wind, and like a huge frog's croak, and like a giant cow's moo—all at once!

"Ooh!" breathed Ruth Ann and Whistle Stick, together.

"Now that shows you what determination and steady practice will do for a person who has a *line*," the Blowster stated with pride. Then he turned his great red eyes toward the two of them and looked them over carefully.

"You're really not bad sorts at all, either of you," he decided after a pause. "I'm honestly sorry for you, but it would certainly be against my rules not to swallow you up or blow you clean away forever, since neither of you does anything worthwhile or even knows what you *might* be able to do."

"But, Mr. Blowster," protested Ruth Ann, "what good would come of that? Then we would never find our **lines** and grow up to do something useful."

"As a matter of fact," added Whistle Stick, "I don't know that I'm in favor of either such fate, at all."

As the two friends stated their opinions, a troubled look came into the Blowster's eyes. "There may be a thread of truth in what you suggest," he said. "I'm a fair-minded being, I hope, and I'll have to admit that the ideas you have expressed have never occurred to me before." He scratched his head reflectively.

Suddenly, Ruth Ann had an idea!

"Mr. Blowster, if you did blow us away, just how would you do it, and where would you send us?"

"Well, I'd blow and blow until you reached the Highest Country on my breath column," said the creature.

"Would it hurt much?" asked Ruth Ann and Whistle Stick together.

"Not one bit," the Blowster assured them, "not one bit. I'd puff and huff and huff and puff until my breath got thick enough to carry you both. Then I'd blow you up to the land behind the littlest star!"

"Is the Highest Country the same as heaven?" asked Ruth Ann, eagerly.

"I'm sure I don't know," replied the Blowster, "but I've heard it said that it's quite a delightful place!"

Ruth Ann clapped her hands.

"Let's go!" she cried. "Perhaps we can find Dukey Daddles!"

"And who is this Dukey Daddles person, if you please?" asked the Blowster, politely.

"Dukey Daddles was my dog," explained Ruth Ann, a little catch coming into her voice. "He was the best friend that I ever had. He got run into heaven by a truck . . . instead of being blown in by a Blowster," she finished.

"Too bad," sympathized the monster. "He would have gotten there quicker by my route. However," he continued, "I'm afraid you'll have to give up all hope of finding Dukey Daddles in the near future. You see, because he's a dog, he wouldn't go to the Highest Country first. He would land in High Country and have to work his way up. There's High Country and the Highest Country. The last, you understand, is where I'm aiming to blow you."

"But look here, Mr. Blowster," said Whistle Stick, who had been thinking while the other two were talking. "It isn't necessary for you to blow us into the Highest Country right away, is it? Why can't you control your breath and blow us first to High Country? Perhaps you could even hold your breath up there long enough for us to see how we liked the place, and if we didn't think much of it, you could inhale us back to Earth.

"Besides, if High Country is where my Dukey Daddles is," cried Ruth Ann, "we might get to see him."

"We might even decide, while visiting up there, what we wanted for our *lines*," Whistle Stick put in persuasively.

"And then, if you were satisfied with the *lines* that we choose, you wouldn't have to do away with us at all, at least not *permanently*." added Ruth Ann.

"Well," said the Blowster hesitantly, "it might work out all right. I'm rather doubtful though, about whether or not you two ought to go wandering about in High Country. I've heard much about the place, and there may be all sorts of dangers up there. Still, if you really want to go, I can certainly get you there!"

"I want to go any place where there's a chance of meeting Dukey Daddles again!" pleaded Ruth Ann.

"How about inhaling us back again if we don't like the place?" asked Whistle Stick, a bit anxiously. "What do you think of that for an idea?"

"Not bad at all," conceded the Blowster. "You relieved my mind by that suggestion. For if while you're away you can decide on *lines* for yourselves, I'd feel justified in not doing away with you both forever."

"Then it's settled," said Ruth Ann.

"Agreed! Now, if you'll take each other's hands and step

to one side for a moment, please," directed the Blowster, "I'll practice a bit until my breath thickens."

Ruth Ann and Whistle Stick joined hands and stepped to one side, where they waited in considerable excitement for the Blowster to get ready.

It was truly terrible to watch the creature! He huffed and he puffed and he puffed and he huffed. At first the two friends could hardly see his breath, but gradually it grew visible, first as a thin cloud, then as a thick white fog.

At last the Blowster shouted, "Get ready!"

His breath swirled and whirled past Ruth Ann and Whistle Stick, like a rolling column of the densest white smoke!

"Before I start to blow and send you off on my breath column," thundered the monster, "I want to tell you about getting back. Take this scale."

Here the Blowster handed Ruth Ann a green scale from his shiny great back.

"Hang it on that chain around your neck. Watch it closely and when it begins to turn black, no matter where you are or what you are doing, you *must* make all possible haste back to the place from where you started. That scale will turn black just before I breathe out the last breath that I will take above Earth tonight. If you are not there to catch it when I inhale for you, I'll have to sink back to the springs in the bowels of the Earth, and you'll have to stay in High Country forever!

Remember now, if you value your lives, don't over-stay your time!"

"We won't," yelled the two, trying to raise their young voices over the terrible whirling and swirling of the Blowster's breath.

"All aboard then!" shouted the monster.

Holding tight to each other's hands, Ruth Ann and Whistle Stick stepped quickly into the thick smoke column. Then at that very instant, they felt themselves lifted and hurled through limitless space!

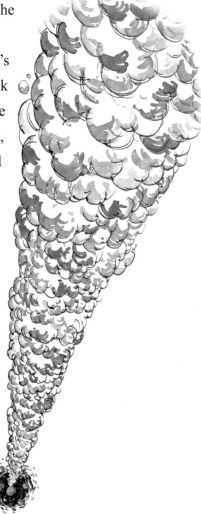

Chapter 6

The High Country

uite suddenly the breath stopped and Ruth Ann and Whistle Stick felt themselves hurled violently forward.

"Well!" gasped Stick, "I guess we've gotten where we're going!"

"It certainly didn't take us long to cover a great distance!" said Ruth Ann, also gasping from their whirling journey through the air. "I wonder what we do now."

The thick white smoke of the Blowster's breath still eddied slowly around them, but the onward motion had ceased entirely. The faint whirlings in the smoke surrounding them were only the last faint signs of the tremendous force that had carried them safely through space. Gradually, even the little eddies of movement stopped. However, the two now found the stationary smoke column so thick that they could not see a foot in front of them. It was only by peering closely that they could make out one another's features.

"What a puzzling place to be!" declared Ruth Ann. "I guess the only thing to do is to try to get our heads out of the Blowster's breath and see where we are. We're absolutely lost now. That's certain! You go that way and I'll go this."

The two friends got up carefully and groped their separate ways, each trying to find the end of the breath column. Ruth Ann soon lost sight of Whistle Stick, but a moment later she heard his voice raised in absolute terror.

"Help!" he shouted. "Help! Ruth Ann, I'm falling!"

As quickly and as cautiously as she could, Ruth Ann made her way in the direction of Whistle Stick's terrified cries. The smoke grew thinner as she neared the edge of the column, and at last she made out the stickman hanging on to the very outer edge!

Ruth Ann reached over to pull her friend up again beside her, when a sight of the space below made her so dizzy that she was forced to close her eyes.

"Don't look down!" warned Whistle Stick. "That's what I did! Keep looking straight at me and then you can help me onto solid breath again. You must be quick though or I shall have to let go. My hands are not used to holding onto anything for any length of time, you know!"

Ruth Ann opened her eyes and found that the dizziness did not return as long as she kept her eyes fast on the face of Whistle Stick. She reached over and caught hold of his branch arms and, gripping them tightly, succeeded in hauling the little fellow back to safety.

"My!" he exclaimed, "What a frightful experience!"

"Wasn't it, though!" Ruth Ann agreed. "You are all atremble! Is there anything I can do for you?"

"I think the best thing for both of us to do," muttered Whistle Stick, "is to find that entrance into High Country, if there is such a place! As long as we stay in this terrible breath, we'll be in constant danger of falling off the edge."

"That's quite true," declared the girl. "The breath only thins out a bit when one is practically falling off. Ugh, did you see how far it was to fall?"

"I should say I did, and the worst part of the whole matter was that I couldn't see any place to fall to! It isn't so terrible to fall if you land somewhere, but just think of falling forever and ever!"

Ruth Ann shuddered in silent agreement.

The friends considered their problem for a moment. At last Whistle Stick broke the silence.

"Neither of us knows just how far around the breath column is," he said. "But if we separate in order to find the way out, one of us may find the entrance into High Country and be unable to make the other hear when he calls."

"You're right," Ruth Ann said. "It seems to me that the best plan for us is to keep together as closely as possible in our search. That way when we find the way in, we'll be able to enter together."

So arm in arm, the two friends fumbled their way into thinner smoke and started slowly around the breath column. Foot by foot, they crept along, not daring to look in any direction but straight ahead, for fear the sight of the vast height above or the limitless depth below would make them dizzy and faint.

Finally, something caught Ruth Ann's eye. It was hanging a short distance beyond them, swaying to and fro at one side of the immovable breath column.

"Look!" she cried. "I don't know just what it is; but it is *something!*"

Quickened by the hope of being able to leave their present dangerous location, the two made their way ahead rapidly to the object they had sighted. Hanging down from somewhere, and almost out of reach from where they stood at the edge of the breath column, was the end of a rope ladder. As it swayed gently to and fro, it swung into the breath column and then out again, quite a distance over the bottomless abyss.

"Oh, dear!" exclaimed Ruth Ann. "It's really terrifying to think of climbing that swaying rope! Do you suppose that can be the entrance into High Country that we have been looking for?"

"Undoubtedly," replied the stick. "It's a certainty that any way out of the Blowster's breath is the only way to get into High Country. We'll simply have to shut our eyes, grab hold, and climb!"

"You catch it first," suggested Ruth Ann, "and let me follow, because your joints aren't working as well as mine, and if you happen to fall, I might be able to catch you and hold you up until you can grab the ropes again."

"Perhaps that way is best," conceded Whistle Stick. "As you say, I'm not working very well yet, and I am light enough that if I fall onto you, I won't knock you off the ropes."

They waited a moment until the ladder swung out and then in again, almost to them. Whistle Stick took a little jump, caught the side ropes in his hands, and went up the ladder one step.

Ruth Ann started to follow and then suddenly stopped, for just as she grabbed for the ladder, it swung out again over the abyss of the space!

Ruth Ann and the Green Blowster

"I'll catch hold next time you swing in," she screamed at Whistle Stick. "I couldn't make it that time."

Whistle Stick's eyes were shut tight, and he was holding on as if his very life depended on it, as indeed it did! Slowly the rope ladder swung into Ruth Ann, and this time she did not hesitate.

"Hurry up a step," she called to Whistle Stick. "Here I come!" Suiting the action to the word, she took hold of the ladder's sides and began to climb upwards.

Rung by rung, the two friends cautiously ascended until suddenly, Stick gave a cry.

"Ouch! I believe we're there," he called back to Ruth Ann. "I bumped my head on something. Yes, it's a little trap door. I'll push on through it and you can follow."

At his words, Ruth Ann dared to open her eyes. She'd had them tightly closed ever since she started the ascent. To be sure, she did not venture to look down even now, only up where a strange sight met her gaze. Through a layer of some substance, a small trap door on brass hinges had been thrown open by Whistle Stick, who had climbed on through and was now peering down at her from above.

"I don't know that I feel much safer on this sort of ground than I did in the Blowster's breath," he grumbled, "but at any rate, it's thick enough so that we can't look through it and see thousands and thousands of miles of sky below us with no place to fall to. Want a hand?"

"No, thank you," replied Ruth Ann. "I can make this quite easily." And she drew herself up through the trap door and into the weirdest looking country that she had ever seen!

"Well," she gasped, in astonishment, "where is everything?"

She and Whistle Stick straightened up and looked over the country. There was absolutely nothing about them for miles on every side, not a tree, not a moving creature, not even a blade of grass! Except for the thin wafer of ground under their feet, they might as well have been suspended in mid-air.

Ruth Ann was disappointed. "So far, I must say that High Country doesn't compare with our dear old Earth."

"And yet," said Whistle Stick, "we can't say that we don't like it because there's nothing not to like!"

Again Ruth Ann nodded her head in silent agreement.

"Let's put down the trap door," she suggested, "and lock it so that no one can get in who is not expected. Then let's set out across this country to see what we can see."

"All right," agreed Whistle Stick, although he seemed rather half-hearted about the idea.

They put down the little door on its brass hinges and started across country.

"You see," said Ruth Ann, "we don't know just how they manage day and night in this land, and it might be just as well for us to get somewhere as quickly as possible, so that if night falls we won't be left out alone in the dark."

"What difference will that make?" said Whistle Stick. "So far as I can see, this High Country is as free of dangers as it is of anything else. Night or day, there's simply nothing up here to be afraid of."

Ruth Ann was about to agree with him, when suddenly far ahead of her, her eye caught sight of a small bit of color. Eagerly she clutched at Whistle Stick's arm.

"Look! Look ahead there!" she cried. "There's a red flag!"

"You'd better not go in that direction then," warned Whistle Stick. "If you remember, red flags on Earth are signs of danger!"

But the girl's mind was made up. She was determined to find out what that bit of red was doing out there in this deserted country. She paid no heed to his warning and walked rapidly forward, her feet twinkling over the dun-colored ground.

At first, poor Whistle Stick tried to prevent her rash conduct by telling her of fearsome experiences on Earth. Careless human beings had been blown to bits by paying no attention to the red flags set as danger signals before great blasts of dynamite. However, walking proved too intense and too new an exercise for him, so finally he gave up his attempts to dissuade Ruth Ann and just walked on beside her, panting heavily from his exertion.

It was not long until the two reached their goal. Once there, they stopped short, overcome with surprise, for just in front of them, balanced on its tail, was a huge snake, wiping the tears from its eyes, with a red bandana handkerchief!

Chapter 7

Lonesome Snake

t was not until Ruth Ann and Whistle Stick gave their audible gasps that the snake realized that he was not alone. He took the handkerchief from his eyes, and a smile of happiness spread over his face as he discovered the newcomers.

"Well," he said, "how good it is to see someone in this dreadful country! I'd just about given up all hope of seeing a living thing again!"

"What are you doing here?" asked Ruth Ann.

"Up to this moment," answered the snake, "I have been crying with loneliness. As I remember it, some fool of a mule stepped on me in a land called Earth, and the next thing I knew, I woke up here in this barren and deserted place, with not even an old moldering log for a snake to sleep under. I was so disappointed that I never even made an effort to move from this place in which I found myself."

"We can't say much for this country ourselves," grumbled Whistle Stick.

"However," cried Ruth Ann, "we're from Earth too, so we're very glad, indeed, to meet someone from the old home."

"Earth's a great place!" exclaimed Lonesome Snake. "I was very fond of it there, although goodness knows folks were sort of down on the whole snake family. How did you get up here? Were you kicked up by a mule?"

"No," Ruth Ann answered. "We were blown in on the breath of the Green Blowster."

"Oooh!" the snake gave quite a shudder. "That horrible creature!"

"We're very fond of him ourselves," declared Ruth Ann. "He was kind to us. He didn't eat us or blow us away for keeps, although he really felt that he ought to. You see, we haven't anything in particular that we want to do on Earth, and the Green Blowster always does away with creatures he meets that don't want to do something worthwhile!"

"How did he happen to let you off?" asked the snake, who was very interested in the little girl's story.

"Well," she explained, "he didn't really let us off. He may blow us away permanently, yet. But we all agreed that if Whistle Stick and I had a short visit to High Country, we might be able to choose a *line* and then return to Earth and do some useful work."

"I see," said Lonesome Snake thoughtfully, "rather a good idea."

"And besides," Ruth Ann said, "I've got a dog called Dukey Daddles who's up here somewhere, and I want to find him. He was run into High Country—by a truck.

"My opinion of dogs isn't the best in the world," remarked Lonesome Snake, "but I was so lonely before you folks came that I do believe I would have been glad to see even your Dukey Daddles."

"May I ask whether or not you are a poisonous reptile?" ventured Whistle Stick, who had been observing the snake with a certain degree of doubtfulness.

Here Lonesome gave the first signs of displeasure. He drew himself up to his full height and replied with considerable dignity.

"As I remarked before," he said, "the whole snake family has been misunderstood by people. Most of us are very respectable, indeed, minding our own business and harming nobody."

"But some snakes do bite with bites that are poisonous." insisted Whistle Stick. "That's an accepted fact."

"Yes," admitted Lonesome, hanging his head in a shamed manner, "there are some of my family who do forget themselves far enough to bite human beings with poison in their fangs. But even most of these misguided relatives of mine give a warning before they strike—like my cousin Riggle Rattlesnake, for instance."

"But surely," said Ruth Ann, "there is some way to tell the good snakes from the bad . . . ?"

"With me it's my tail, my dear," answered Lonesome, pausing for an instant to regard his extremity with pride. "Any snake with a beautifully tapering tail, like mine, is sure to belong to one of our very best families. A snake with such a tail is always a perfect gentleman and absolutely harmless!"

"What a great relief!" exclaimed Whistle Stick. "I never do believe in taking unnecessary risks!"

Again Lonesome began to bristle.

Upon seeing this, Ruth Ann, anxious to avoid trouble between her companions, quickly broke into the conversation.

"Let's have a conference," she suggested, "and see what we'll do in this dreadful country."

Whistle Stick slowly shook his head. "There's not an idea

in my brain," he confessed. "I'll have to take time and think up a few."

"What do you think we had better do, Lonesome?" asked Ruth Ann.

"Any decision you make will be all right with me," answered the snake, "except that I do not want to be left alone again. It's a terrible feeling!" At the memory of his homesickness, great tears welled up in Lonesome's eyes and he was forced to use his red bandana to wipe them from his cheeks.

"I agree with Lonesome to that extent," declared Whistle Stick. "I believe that we ought to stand or fall together. Whatever danger there may be in this country, let us share it!"

"That's settled then," said Ruth Ann. It was good to see her new friends agreeing. "Now let's start out and see what there is to see. The quicker we get under way, the sooner we find Dukey Daddles!"

"Of course, I shall take my bandana with me," the snake decided as he carefully tightened his handkerchief with his tail. "In a country like this, one never knows what may happen, and it is such a convenient thing to cry into!"

"We mustn't expect trouble," said Ruth Ann cheerfully. "I fail to see anything at all to worry us."

"It's not always the dangers we see that are the worst, but as you say, let's get started," mumbled Whistle Stick. "If you will go ahead, Ruth Ann, as a sort of scout, Lonesome and I will bring up the rear."

So the three friends set out over the thin ground without much hope of discovering anything or anybody. Steadily they walked until Ruth Ann's feet grew so tired that she feared they might drop off from fatigue. And still, there was the same thin, dun-colored layer of ground under them and the same light height of sky over their heads. Not a sprig of green, not a flying bird, not a little creeping animal broke the silent barrenness of the view.

Then at last, when the trio had almost abandoned all hope, they saw what looked like the very end of the country. Lonesome noticed it first.

"Do look!" he shouted. "Here we've walked and walked and all to no purpose. Yonder is the Jumping Off Place!"

Sure enough, when Whistle Stick and Ruth Ann looked in the direction in which the snake pointed, High Country seemed to come to an abrupt end. For a space ahead of them, the ground stretched out as bare and uninhabited as ever, but then it fell off abruptly into the blue depths of space, and apparently there was nothing further. They had reached the very end of this new world!

"There must be more to High Country than what we have seen," Ruth Ann cried with a little shudder, for she could feel herself dropping off the edge of the land, just as Whistle Stick had fallen off the Blowster's breath. "We know that Dukey

Daddles is up here someplace and I'm going on anyway—up to the very edge!"

"Do have a care!" warned Whistle Stick. But he had no chance to finish, at least not to Ruth Ann, for she was already walking ahead and Stick and Lonesome had to hurry their steps to keep up with her.

After a short while of walking, Ruth Ann discovered that what they had thought was the end of High Country was in reality only the top of a steep incline. She turned toward Lonesome and Stick, who were hurriedly approaching, and called out to them cheerfully.

"It's all right, friends! It isn't the Jumping Off Place! It's only the top of a steep hill, and I believe I can see a woodland down below in a little valley!"

The little girl sat down on the edge of the incline to rest for a moment until the two friends came blowing and puffing up to her.

"I'm glad that there's still something to look forward to," said the snake between puffs.

"And particularly that there is a woodland in the distance," added Whistle Stick, quite brightly for him. "I ought to feel quite at home in the woods."

Here Ruth Ann pointed out what seemed to be the dim outlines of a forest far below them in the valley. It seemed to extend almost to the foot of the hill at the summit of which they were standing.

"I don't know about you," she exclaimed, "but I have a splendid idea for getting down there in the quickest possible time. I'm going to use this steep incline like a playground slide and slide right down to the forest!"

"It doesn't seem like a proper way to travel," said Lonesome, rather critically, "but I dare say it's rapid." He spread out his red bandana carefully to share and seated himself upon it at the very edge of the slope, preparing for their downward flight.

"I'd hate to lose any of my arms and legs now that they work," complained Whistle Stick, "and it is a bit risky undertaking this, but I'll confess that I'm so tired of walking that I'm ready for anything else." So he sat down beside Ruth Ann and Lonesome.

"Are we all ready?" shouted Ruth Ann. Seeing that her friends were indeed prepared, she added:

"Ready! Set! Go!"

At the signal, the three pushed themselves over the edge of the incline and sped down the steep slope as swift and true as an arrow. At last they came to the bottom and stopped with a sharp jerk!

"If that hill had been any steeper," Ruth Ann exclaimed, "and that slope had been any longer, I'd have lost my breath entirely!" She proceeded to pick her own arms and legs out of the medley that they made as they sprawled over one another at the foot of the hill.

"That was a very ungentlemanly proceeding," remarked Lonesome as he righted himself and retied his bandana. "But it did accomplish its purpose. Here we are!"

"Where is here?" asked Whistle Stick. "Where are we?" He was still dazed, so Ruth Ann went to him and patted him gently on the back.

"That was an experience for you, being alive such a short time," she comforted. "Do you feel better now?"

He shook his head mournfully. "I doubt if I shall ever be quite the same again," he stated with conviction. "But my mind is clearing up a trifle. There was some talk of a forest, I believe . . ."

"Oh, yes," cried Ruth Ann. "I was so excited over the slide that for a moment I'd forgotten the forest!"

At one and the same time, all three friends faced about and looked in the direction in which they had seen the woods from the top of the steep incline.

"Why, what very peculiar trees!" exclaimed Ruth Ann.

"Indeed, yes," agreed Whistle Stick and Lonesome, in astonished tones.

Hurriedly the three approached the trees. Ruth Ann stretched out her hand to touch one, but her hand and arm went right through the trunk and out the opposite side!

"They're nothing but shadows!" she said in amazement. "Who ever heard tell of such a thing?"

"I think I can explain them," said Lonesome importantly. "You've heard of shade trees, of course?"

"Why, yes," answered Ruth Ann. "Shade trees are common on Earth. We call them shade trees because of the comfortable shadows that they throw."

"Then that explains this forest," declared the snake. "These are the shadows that some of the shade trees have thrown. They've simply thrown these shadows too far and they've landed up here in High Country."

"That snake is talking utter nonsense, if you ask me," muttered Whistle Stick, in disgust.

"Well, whatever they are, what are we going to do with

them now that we've found them?" asked Ruth Ann, almost in tears. "I was hoping so hard that we had found a real forest with perhaps some little woodsy creatures in it and red berries, too. A forest like this doesn't do us any good."

"Oh," comforted Lonesome. "I wouldn't say that. We can get right inside one of these shadows to rest for a time. It must be quite comfortably dark on the inside of a shadow tree. We can make believe that it's night and have a good nap. There's only one thing that I'd like to ask of *you*," Snake addressed Whistle Stick.

"When we're settling down for our nap," said Snake, "will you let me coil up under you? Then I can make believe that you are a log, and it will be so much like home!"

At the last word, tears welled up again in the snake's eyes and he wiped them away with his red bandana, half apologetically this time.

"Well, I guess you can," consented Whistle Stick slowly, "but mind you now, that you don't wiggle around any and disturb me while I'm trying to rest."

The snake promised perfect quiet, so the three friends picked out the biggest shadow that they could find, one that had been thrown by an enormous oak, and crept inside of it to nap for a time and rest from their long walk. Little did they dream of the danger that was, even then, hovering over their heads!

Chapter 8

Attack by the Enemy Birds

or some time, there was absolute quiet in Shadow Forest. The three friends were sleeping peacefully in the gray shade of the great oak. Tired out by their long walk and by the exciting slide down the steep cliff, none of them moved a bit in their deep slumber. Ruth Ann's breath rose and fell gently. Lonesome Snake, coiled up under Whistle Stick, was almost invisible. Stick himself, with legs and arms sprawled out in every direction, was enjoying to the fullest his very first real sleep. He had been unable to close his eyelids at all before Ruth Ann had rubbed them with growing grease.

As the three rested, an ominous black speck appeared in the east. Marring the clear sky of High Country, it grew larger and larger as it approached Shadow Forest, where the friends slept on, unconscious of any ill likely to befall them.

As the black spot neared the forest, it took more definite

shape. It swelled into a great triangular cloud of flying birds who were evidently on their way to the shade trees. As they drew ever nearer, a great chattering and twittering arose and penetrated into the shadow of the great oak where Ruth Ann and her companions had taken refuge.

The little girl heard it first and nudged Whistle Stick, who woke from sleep with a start.

"Do you hear anything?" she asked him, nervously. "It sounds to me like the chattering of wild birds in the thicket down beside the pool."

"This seems to come from overhead," he whispered back.

"I guess I'll get out of this shade and see if I can find out what is making all the racket," she declared. "I can't stand suspense!"

"You'd better not," warned the stick. "If you take my advice, you'll lie perfectly still until you see exactly what it is that's making all the noise."

"Perhaps that is more sensible," agreed Ruth Ann. So she sat tensely motionless and waited.

A few moments later the great cloud of birds descended upon Shadow Forest. They were all sorts and colors: little yellow birds like canaries; bigger birds with brown backs and red breasts like robins; and middle-sized birds like black birds whose feathers glistened like ink in sunlight. They all carried slingshots and small bags of pebbles and wore scowls on their faces. They were all in a very bad humor.

One of the birds, a woodpecker whom the others called Wingus, seemed to be in command. He also carried a slingshot and pebbles for ammunition, but he was dressed in a small plug hat and an opera cape that gave him an air of great distinction.

He lit on the ground, not a great distance from the large oak shadow wherein the three friends were sleeping. The other birds quickly arranged themselves about him on low shadow branches, some of them standing on the ground in large circular rows. Wingus was obviously going to make a speech.

"Attention followers!" he proceeded with a grand wave of his right wing. "Again we have returned to Shadow Forest without satisfying our desire for vengeance!"

Here all the birds interrupted with expressions of disappointment. It was a moment or two before the chattering died down sufficiently for the leader to make himself heard.

"You all know why we are here! We have been forced from Earth by the slingshots of little boys, and we have sworn to even the score by stoning with our pebbles of revenge any little boys that we find wandering about up here!"

At these words, another tumult of chatter and twitter arose from the birds.

"Boys, bad luck to them all! Down with the whole tribe!" they shouted in unison.

Ruth Ann looked at Whistle Stick and shuddered.

"How bloodthirsty they are," she whispered, so as not to

be overheard. "I never imagined that a bird could have such cruel thoughts!"

"Well," the stick answered, "we can hardly blame them. It must be annoying to be forced into High Country by boys who shot you just for fun."

"I suppose it is, but it is too bad that a bird is able to go around carrying pebbles of revenge. It's as much as our lives are worth to venture out among such an army of enemies. They would certainly attack us at once!"

She had hardly gotten the words out of her mouth when a most unlucky thing happened. Lonesome, who had remained sound asleep during the advent of the Enemy Birds, stirred suddenly and raised his head a trifle. Whistle Stick, under whom he was coiled, tilted forward with the snake's sudden motion and pitched head first out from within the shade of the great oak.

Instantly a great hubbub arose among the birds who flew screeching about poor old Whistle Stick.

"A boy! A boy!" they chirped out in great glee. "At last a boy has been delivered into our hands!"

Wingus, who had reached the stick man first and had looked him over, silenced them with another wave of the wing.

"It's not a boy!" he stated with certainty. "I do not recognize him as anything that I have ever seen upon Earth."

The rest of the birds flew back a short distance with disappointed twitterings.

From their shelter within the shadow of the great oak, Ruth Ann and Lonesome, who had awakened from all the commotion, watched their friend anxiously.

Whistle Stick, however, was facing Wingus and his army of Enemy Birds with absolute fearlessness.

"I am not a boy. I am Whistle Stick," he introduced himself proudly. "Once upon a time, I was a whistle and I belonged to a little boy, and I'm proud of it. I love little boys!"

At this brave statement, angry chatterings swelled from the birds, this time louder than ever before.

"Hear! Hear!" they shouted. "He loves little boys! Down with Whistle Stick!"

Fluttering their wings angrily, the crowd of birds led by Wingus swooped down upon the courageous Whistle Stick. Half jostling, half pushing, they forced him to take a stand in front of one of the shadow trees. Then at an order from Wingus, two of the birds bound him hand and foot with coarse twine from their knapsacks. The others, with exclamations of delight, flew to some distance in front of him where they began to take stones from their ammunition bags and fit them to their slingshots.

"Oh," breathed Ruth Ann, in terror, "what a brutal thing to do!"

The intention of the Enemy Birds was at once apparent.

They were about to make a game out of the stick's helplessness. Bound, he was unable to move and they were going to use him as a target for their sport!

"Poor old fellow!" said Lonesome. "He's a bit of a grouch, but a good fellow for all of that. I'm afraid he's done for!"

"He isn't—if I can help it!" cried Ruth Ann. Without a thought for herself, she ran out from the oak shadow to try to rescue her friend.

At her sudden appearance, the birds uttered cries of alarm. Then as soon as they saw who it was, they crowded about her, making Shadow Forest hideous with their screeches of violent intentions.

"It's a girl!" they shouted, led by Wingus. "It's a girl! Girls are friends of little boys! We know girls! Down with little girls!"

Gleefully, they crowded around poor Ruth Ann as she tried to reach her friend. They pushed and jostled her until they forced her up against a tree beside Whistle Stick. There they tied her securely. They flew back, chattering gaily, and took their places in preparation for their cruel sport.

"Thank you for coming to my rescue," whispered Whistle Stick, in appreciation. "You'll have to excuse me for not looking at you when I'm speaking to you, but I'm tied so securely that I can't move even an eighth of an inch. It's as bad as it was before you rubbed me with growing grease."

"I can't move a bit either," she replied. "I'm sorry that I couldn't really help you, but I just couldn't stay behind in that tree shadow and see these horrible birds hurt you without at least trying to save you. Remember, the three of us agreed to stand or fall, together!"

Here their conversation was interrupted by another great commotion among the birds. A glance in the direction of the winged army, and the two captives understood what the trouble was. Each of the birds wished to be the first to shoot a stone at the helpless victims. They wore such cruel and heartless expressions that Ruth Ann couldn't repress a shudder.

"Look here," said Wingus, attempting to quiet his followers, "you can't all be first. Suppose I count out the birds who will have the first twelve shots. If our captives are still alive after that, I'll count out another twelve to finish them off!"

Shouts arose. "That's good! All right! Wingus, count out!"

Apparently the birds had met the suggestion of their leader with approval.

Quickly they arranged themselves in a great circle and Wingus proceeded quite solemnly to count out the first twelve birds to shoot at the captives.

Pointing his wing first at one bird, then at the next, Wingus chanted:

Point at one,

Point at two,

Who will lead the bout?

Hurdy-gurdy,

Lucky birdie,

You . . . are . . . out!

At last, the lucky twelve were chosen and they stepped proudly forward, facing the hapless two at a distance of about twenty paces. They began to take pebbles from their bags while the other birds regarded them with envy.

"Now when I say 'one!' have your slings and pebbles ready," ordered Wingus. "When I say 'two!' take aim, and at 'three!' fire!"

Ruth Ann wiggled uncomfortably. "It wouldn't be so bad," she confessed, "if we knew where the first shot was going to hit. Suppose they hit us in the eye!"

"Or in the nose!" Whistle Stick winced.

"Well," stated Ruth Ann, "I do wish they'd start! It's terrible standing here waiting and imagining such frightful things!"

As if in answer to her wish, Wingus marched to one side of the birds chosen for the first firing line and made a motion with his wing.

"One!" he counted. At his signal the birds set their pebbles in their slings.

"Two!" came the next order.

Ruth Ann saw the birds raise their slings and closed her eyes before the hailstorm of pebbles that she knew would follow.

Suddenly, an intense and dreadful quiet descended upon the forest. Even with her eyes closed, she knew that something had happened. When she ventured to look out again upon the birds, an amazing spectacle met her sight!

The firing squad still stood like statues with slings upraised, but now, instead of taking aim at the captives, they were staring in horror at something near the feet of Ruth Ann and Whistle Stick.

At first glance, Ruth Ann could not see the cause of the birds' terror. She soon understood though, for slithering out from under her feet came Lonesome Snake hissing angrily, his eyes glaring at Wingus and his tail bound tightly with the red bandana handkerchief!

Chapter 9

The Rescue

ith a sinuous glide that was fascinating to see, Lonesome Snake drew near the leader of the bird army. As if hypnotized, cruel Wingus could not take his eyes away from those of the avenging serpent.

"What is Lonesome going to do?" said Ruth Ann.

"I'm not sure," said Whistle Stick, "but while lying so long in the woods, I did hear the forest folk mention a peculiar power that snakes have. It seems that if snakes stare at birds steadily, the birds are at last overpowered by the evil glare in their eyes and are forced to flutter closer and closer until the reptiles are able to seize and devour them!"

"Oh!" gasped Ruth Ann. "What a terrible fate for Wingus!"

"Serves him jolly well right if you ask me," stated the stick. "I have never put in such an uncomfortable time in my life. I think these terrible birds deserve a lesson!"

"I suppose they do," agreed Ruth Ann finally, although she could not help feeling sorry for anything that was to suffer such a terrible fate.

Slowly the snake approached Wingus. As he realized that the end was in store for him, the courage of the bird leader gave way and he collapsed pitifully. Unable to take his eyes from those of the advancing snake, he began to tremble violently. His opera hat tumbled from his head. His slingshot fell from under his faltering wing. He took a feeble step toward Lonesome, who had stopped his graceful glide, but whose eyes were still fixed on Wingus with a baleful glare.

As their leader began his stumbling advance toward the snake, the birds began to moan. Evidently they realized

his utter helplessness.

"Mercy! Mercy!" begged Wingus feebly, as he felt himself drawn irresistibly into the jaws of the great serpent.

The scene was too much for Ruth Ann's tender heart!

"Lonesome!" she called. "Don't eat Wingus! Cruel as he has been, let him go this time for my sake!"

"Don't be foolish," grunted Whistle Stick. "If Lonesome does let him go, we'll never get out of this forest alive! These birds can be very treacherous, indeed. I should think you would have learned that by this time."

Obviously Lonesome shared the little man's opinion with regard to the Enemy Birds, for he did not alter his plan by a turn of the head. Unheeding the pleas of Wingus for mercy, he stared steadily at the woodpecker until it crept with faltering steps to within reaching distance of the serpent's jaws. Then with a flash of his head, the snake seized his feathered victim and gulped and swallowed until cruel Wingus disappeared down the reptile's cavernous throat!

"Well, so much for Mr. Wingus," commented Whistle Stick, unsympathetically. "Now, I hope Lonesome remembers that we're still tightly bound and can't move hand or foot to help ourselves."

"Ugh!" Ruth Ann shuddered, still worrying over the fate of Wingus. "I think Lonesome might have taken some other course to rescue us that wasn't so bloodthirsty."

"I daresay you'll feel sorrier for that snake than for Wingus before long," said Whistle Stick. "As tough a morsel as that bird leader is, he will likely give our well-bred snake indigestion."

Here the attention of the two friends was again centered upon the great serpent. He was advancing majestically upon the rest of the bird army, transfixing it with his powerful glance. The army was retreating in horror. Suddenly Lonesome stopped and spoke in a loud, clear voice:

"Birds! You have dared to attack two beings lately arrived from Earth. Unless you unbind my friends at once and allow us to proceed unharmed upon our way, I shall force you, each and every one, to share the fate of your leader, Wingus!"

At Lonesome's words there arose a chorus of frightened cries from the birds. It was clear that they were absolutely under the domination of the snake, who wiggled his length ferociously to add to their terror.

"Release my friends at once!" he ordered.

Uttering pitiful twitters, the whole bird army rose and flew to the place where Ruth Ann and Whistle Stick were tied. There they pushed and shoved one another, all trying to unbind their victims and thus win the good graces of their conqueror, the snake.

In a moment the bonds of the little girl and her fellow captive were loosened, and the two stood as free as they had been when they entered the forest. The birds flew a few feet away and huddled there together in a frightened group, watching the snake as it glided to the side of its friends.

"Well," Lonesome asked, proudly, "what do you think of me as a strategist?"

"I think you're wonderful!" exclaimed Ruth Ann, jumping about to enjoy her freedom.

"You're not bad," conceded Whistle Stick gruffly, as he rubbed his joints stiffened by his period of enforced inactivity.

"Just think what would have happened to us if we hadn't met Lonesome at all!" continued Ruth Ann.

Whistle Stick shuddered in answer.

"Of course, I can't help feeling sorry for Wingus. Is he digested yet?" asked Ruth Ann. "And why have you got the bandana around your tail?"

"Don't you remember what he said about his being quite harmless?" whispered Whistle Stick in Ruth Ann's ear. "He's got the handkerchief on to fool the birds about his tail. He wants them to think he's poisonous!"

"Sssss . . . ssss!" hissed the snake. "Not so loud! We're not out of danger yet by any means, and we won't be until we can get away from these birds. They're all ears!"

He turned fiercely on the huddled birds and addressed them.

"Be gone, Enemy Birds, to the highest branches!"

In response to the snake's order, the birds arose from

the ground and with shrill chatterings flew to the tops of the shadow trees where they perched, trembling with fear.

"Quick now!" whispered Lonesome tensely. "Let's waste no time and hurry away as fast as we can. There's no telling what may pop into the minds of those harum-scarum birds. They're likely to do anything!"

Ruth Ann walked swiftly ahead, with Lonesome and Whistle Stick following closely behind. The farther they walked, the denser grew the shadow trees. Finally, they were stumbling right through the trees in their effort to find a way out. At last Ruth Ann sank to the floor of the forest, absolutely tired out.

"I don't seem to be able to make one foot move ahead of the other anymore," she gasped, "and I do believe that the Blowster's scale is already turning a shade darker green. At this rate, we will never find Dukey Daddles before we have to turn back!"

"I know that I can't go on any further," panted Whistle Stick. "This walking business is too much for my fresh joints."

"I don't see that we're getting anywhere! That's the big trouble," complained Ruth Ann. "Here we've been walking for a long time and apparently are not any nearer the edge of the forest than we were when we started."

"Instead, we seem to be getting farther into it," commented Lonesome. "I've noticed that the growth of trees is getting thicker instead of thinner as we walk along. As long as we stay in the forest, we're apt to have trouble with those Enemy Birds!"

Discouraged, the trio looked about them. The shadow trees, some large, some small, stood close about them like giant ghosts with pale gray arms. The light was dim now and the forest presented a weird and impenetrable aspect. For some moments they sat in gloomy silence. At last Lonesome broke the stillness:

"As a usual thing I wouldn't be so tired myself," he said, apologetically, "but I haven't eaten that abominable Wingus yet. He's a lot of extra weight to carry around!"

Ruth Ann let out a cry of happy surprise!

"Do you mean that Wingus is still alive inside of you?" she gasped.

"Still alive and kicking," replied the snake. "Look and see!"

Sure enough as Ruth Ann examined the long throat of Lonesome more closely, it was quite easy to make out the outlines of the bird leader who was still fluttering away in the snake's body.

"Why, you swallowed him whole!" expressed Ruth Ann with delight.

"Yes," nodded Lonesome with pride, "and I don't mind telling you that it's a very difficult trick!"

"Oh!" cried Ruth Ann, clapping her hands. "I can't help

being glad that Wingus is alive, even though he was cruel to us."

An idea presented itself suddenly to her. She turned quickly to her friends and exclaimed excitedly:

"Why, don't you see? The fact that Wingus is alive after all gives us a way we can possibly escape."

Her friends continued to gaze at her blankly.

"You'll agree with me after I explain it to you," she went on. "If you'd ever heard about Jonah and the whale, you'd have thought of it yourselves. Lonesome can spit out Wingus, just as the whale spat out Jonah, in the Bible story. Then Wingus can lead us out of the forest. He must know every tree in it!"

As she finished, both Lonesome and Whistle Stick looked at her in admiration.

"It sounds as if it would work," agreed the stick man. "We can certainly try it anyway—that is, if Lonesome is willing."

"I have only one thing to add," said the snake. "One of you had better put a hand down my throat and grasp Wingus firmly about his wings, so that he will not be able to fly away and marshal another attack upon us from which we shall not so easily escape."

Ruth Ann looked at Stick as Lonesome finished. It seemed to her that he looked frightened at the serpent's suggestion, so she spoke up quickly herself.

"All right, Lonesome," she said bravely. "I'll put my hand

down your throat and get a firm hold on Wingus. Then I'll bring him up in such a tight grip that he'll never get away."

"Good girl," cheered the snake. "I do believe Whistle Stick is afraid of me—after all I've done for him, too." Lonesome added this last remark a bit reproachfully.

"Not at all! Not at all!" broke in Whistle Stick, hastily clearing his throat. "But I never take unnecessary chances!"

"Well, it doesn't matter," said Lonesome, a bit coldly. "Ruth Ann has agreed to bring Wingus back again to the light of day, so we don't need your help. Now I'll open my jaws as far as possible," he continued, addressing the girl, "and then you'll be able to reach Wingus quite easily."

As the great serpent opened its mouth for a second time, Ruth Ann could hardly repress a shiver. Still, she was brave and approached the snake. Hesitating only the slightest instant, she thrust her hand and arm into the reptile's mouth and down its cavernous throat.

She felt the feathered body of the bird leader flutter under her fingers. Slowly she tightened her hand in a grasp about his body and pinioned his wings to his sides. She drew him carefully out of Lonesome's mouth and held him triumphantly over her head so that her two friends might see him.

Proud Wingus had undergone a pitiful change. His feathers were soggy and wilted from his stay in the dark recesses of the snake's throat, and his cruel little eyes had changed from the arrogant eyes of a commander to those of a frightened captive. He looked first at one, then at another of the friends, in a mute appeal for mercy.

"Ah!" taunted Lonesome, "how proud Wingus has fallen!"

"He doesn't look so much like a dude now that his tall hat and opera cloak are gone," grunted Whistle Stick.

Ruth Ann's kind heart could not stand their mean-spirited words. "You mustn't talk to him so!" she scolded. "Tell him that we have decided to be merciful to him!"

At this, the poor bird lifted his head with the light of hope in his eyes.

"You mean that you aren't going to eat me, after all?" he asked, addressing himself to the snake.

Lonesome reflected a moment and then replied, "I confess that I have not made my mind up for certain, though I suppose that it is only reasonable to let you go free, provided you agree to help us out of our difficulty."

"You see, we're lost," explained Whistle Stick.

"And we want you to lead us out of Shadow Forest," finished Ruth Ann. "If you do that for us, we'll let you go back to your bird army, provided you won't let them attack us again."

"It shall make me very happy to serve such a kind-hearted child as yourself," agreed Wingus, perking up and looking very happy for sure. "I shall guide you and protect you from my birds."

Just as he finished speaking, the woodpecker wiggled himself free from the little girl's restraining hand and flew far above the friends to the tops of the trees.

"Now you've done it!" scolded Whistle Stick, half-angry that she had allowed the bird to escape.

The remaining trio raised anxious eyes to the sky, where high over the trees circled the escaped captive.

"I daresay we'll never see that bird again." asserted Lonesome.

But even as he spoke, Wingus swooped down from above like a miniature airplane and poised himself lightly on a branch near their heads.

"Sorry to worry you," he chirped, "but I felt sure that if I had asked your permission to do that, you would not have given it, and I simply had to get above the tree tops in order to find out where we are."

Ruth Ann nodded that she understood.

"I knew that we could rely on you," she sighed. "You look like a bird that would keep his promise."

Wingus preened himself proudly at that.

"I have a plan for leading you all out of the forest safely," he said. "I hope it will suit you. You see, in order to see constantly that we are going in the proper direction, I shall have to fly at a height far above your heads. It will be awkward for you to keep your heads in the air watching me, so I suggest that I pluck a certain number of my feathers and keep dropping them, one by one, as I fly. Thus, by looking at the ground underfoot, you will be able to find a path of feathers that will lead you to the edge of the forest!"

Ruth Ann clapped her hands in approval of the scheme and both Lonesome and Whistle Stick looked at Wingus with a new respect in their eyes.

"Your plan should work admirably," complimented the snake. "Let's get started at once."

The woodpecker rose swiftly into the air and, circling once or twice above their heads, started in a line almost at right angles to the one in which the friends had been proceeding. Hurriedly, the three followed. They had no difficulty whatever in finding their way, for every foot or two Wingus had dropped one of his glistening black feathers, and it showed up like a blot of ink on the light-colored floor of High Country. It seemed hardly any time at all until the trees began to thin out. Finally, with shouts of triumph, the friends emerged from the ghostly shadows.

Wingus joined them at once from his height in the sky.

"You'll let me go now, I'm sure," he said. "I've kept my part of the bargain and led you safely out of Shadow Forest. I'd like to be going back to my birds for they will be worrying about me."

"Oh, Wingus, before you go," said Ruth Ann, eagerly, "have you seen a dog wandering about High Country—a dog who answers to the name of Dukey Daddles?"

"No, I haven't," replied Wingus. "As far as I know, there isn't a dog wandering about up here at all."

As Ruth Ann turned away to hide her disappointment, the bird addressed himself to Lonesome.

"For a fact you are the only reptile I've ever seen in High Country," he said. "If you could forget the unfortunate circumstances of our meeting, I should like to welcome you in the name of the Enemy Birds and myself. A forest isn't a forest without at least one snake," Wingus added plaintively.

"Couldn't we persuade you to live here with us in Shadow Forest?"

"Well, not at present," replied Lonesome, although he was pleased and flattered at the invitation. "I've promised Ruth Ann and Whistle Stick to join them in their search for Dukey Daddles. I will, however, think your offer over and perhaps . . . sometime . . . ."

With mutual expressions of good will, the three bade goodbye to Wingus. They watched him fly again to the height of sky above them, and circling about to get his bearings, Wingus set out finally, straight back into the interior of the forest and his feathered following.

Chapter 10

Loppy Wallops

fter Wingus had disappeared, the three friends stared at one another inquiringly.

"Well, danger is over from Shadow Forest and the Enemy Birds!" announced Ruth Ann.

"But it's not much use being rescued if there is nothing to be rescued for," observed Lonesome, sagely.

"You never spoke a truer word," grumbled Whistle Stick. "Whether we're alive or not, it's beginning to be hard for me to see the use of anything."

"Oh, Whistle Stick," cried Ruth Ann, "don't be disheartened. You haven't had half a chance . . . what with being in such danger so soon after you came alive!"

"Don't waste any sympathy on him," put in the snake. "He's a born grumbler, that stick! Ever since I met him he's been grouching about something. He hasn't even average politeness," continued Lonesome as he repositioned his red bandana to its proper place.

"Will you mind your own business!" Whistle Stick exploded. "I guess I know a few manners without being taught etiquette by a snake!"

Ruth Ann, distressed by the quarrelsome tone of her friends, laid one little hand on a shoulder of each.

"Do you know," she confessed, "I don't think High Country is half bad. There's really a lovely light here and . . . "

"Yes, a lovely light," interrupted Whistle Stick sarcastically, "and beautiful birds, beautiful birds that like nothing better than shooting you full of holes with their stone pebbles!"

"Will you be still," muttered Lonesome. "If you keep on thinking such disagreeable thoughts, you'll wish bad luck on us as sure as anything!"

"We can't have any worse luck than we've had," commented Whistle Stick. "Can we now? I ask you."

"We aren't in any particular danger that we know of," Ruth Ann put in gently. "And Wingus is a friend now. I just feel sure that everything is coming out all right!"

Even as she spoke so hopefully, a fearful hubbub of some-one shouting to them from a distance came to their ears.

"Do you hear that?" cried Ruth Ann. "What do you sup-pose it is? What could it be?"

"It's probably some dreadful creature that will finish us off entirely," grunted Whistle Stick. "It certainly sounds excited enough to do anything!"

At first look in the direction whence the cries came, the three friends made out nothing unusual. As their eyes became accustomed to the vague distance, a little figure grew plain to them. It was running toward them at great speed, and at intervals, it gave rise to loud blood-curdling yells.

"What a peculiar looking creature!" exclaimed Ruth Ann as it drew nearer. "Do you suppose it means to harm us?"

"What difference if it does?" asked Whistle Stick. "There's no place for us to hide and nothing we can use for a weapon against it, anyway."

"Keep still, grumbler!" ordered Lonesome. "Perhaps it's close enough now to make out what it's yelling about."

The huddled trio stood very still and listened with all their might to the cries that were issuing from the strange being who was approaching them on the run.

The shouts were unintelligible at first, but soon words became clear.

"To the hills! To the hills!" the creature was screaming. "Flee for your lives!"

The being was well up to them now, and in spite of its terrifying message, Ruth Ann and her friends could not help being amused by its strange appearance.

The creature was short, its head barely on level with Whistle Stick's. Its head was small for the rest of it and shaped somewhat like the head of a pin. It was dressed in green trousers and a red coat with huge brass buttons, and it walked with a sideways motion, carrying its right shoulder high in the air. In its hand it carried a stout wooden club.

It was obviously thoroughly frightened and kept right on shouting its words into the very faces of the puzzled friends.

"Waste not a moment! Flee! Flee to the hills!" It repeated its warning, throwing its arms about in a frenzy.

"Why must we flee?" questioned Ruth Ann. "Tell us why!"

At her words, the fright of the creature increased. "You'll know why all too soon, if you do not obey me!" it cried, still flinging its arms about. "Ask no more questions, but flee! We have no time for words until we reach the safety of the hills!"

Since Ruth Ann and her friends refused to become alarmed, the creature began to push them ahead with its hands, talking rapidly.

"Hurry! Hurry, all of you! You have no idea of the terrible

fate that will overtake you if you do not move. You are in the path of the greatest danger. At this very moment we must make it to the hills! At once!"

Some of the real fright in the creature's voice penetrated at last into the hearts of Ruth Ann and her friends. They allowed themselves to break into a run at the command of the odd being, making for the distant hills with all possible speed.

They ran, and they ran, and they ran. Over the thin, dun-colored floor of High Country they ran! They ran so fast that not one of them had breath for a word. They ran, and the wind of High Country sang past their ears like an echo of the great Blowster's breath. They ran, and they ran.

At first the tiny creature who had warned them was well in the lead. As the rapid pace kept up, Ruth Ann, Whistle Stick, and Lonesome came up abreast and held the pace with him. Whistle Stick groaned with the pain of his joints, and even Ruth Ann and the snake gasped for breath.

They ran, and they ran, and they ran some more until at last, with sighs of relief, they found themselves at the foot of the first range of hills. They puffed breathlessly up the trail toward the summit.

"Now, I'll answer your questions," panted the creature, as they all sank down gasping on the top of the highest peak. "I guess we're safe now—even from that awful Incorrigible River!"

"Incorrigible River?" said Ruth Ann, breathlessly. "What is the Incorrigible River and *who* are you!"

"I am Loppy Wallops, the Pinhead, and Guardian of the Incorrigible River," gasped the creature. "And what a terrible job it is! It's my business to keep the river in its banks. Usually I'm rather successful, but lately River has been swelling so high that the stout cudgel I have for walloping it back to within its boundaries has no effect upon it at all! Any moment now, I expect to see it come rolling through the opening you can see there between those two ranges of hills and flood this entire valley!"

"What is this Incorrigible River, anyway?" asked Lonesome, between gasping breaths. "How did it happen? Did rain cause it to swell?"

"Rain?" Loppy Wallops seemed puzzled. "What's rain? I never heard of rain before."

"Rain is wet," answered Whistle Stick, breaking into the conversation. "Rain, I remember distinctly, is wet—and disagreeable."

"Well," Loppy Wallops reflected, "the Incorrigible River is wet all right, so he might be made of rain as far as his wetness goes, but he certainly is not disagreeable. He's the jolliest river you ever saw. He's always laughing!"

"Jolly?" exclaimed Ruth Ann. "Why, if he's jolly, he'll not drown us. A jolly river couldn't do a thing like that!"

"He's jolly all right," repeated Loppy Wallops with conviction.

"You can see yourselves how lopsided I am! I got this way hitting that terrible river with my cudgel and even when I'd wallop him the hardest, he'd always laugh and joke at me. He's jolly all right; he is!"

"And as to his drowning us, you know we can be drowned just as well by a jolly river as by a grumbly one," stated Whistle Stick with considerable sadness in his voice. "I, for one, am glad that we're high in the hills instead of back there on the flat country."

Just as Whistle Stick finished speaking, a great roaring reached their ears.

"What did I tell you! We had no time to waste!" gasped Loppy Wallops, triumphantly. "Look there!"

The three friends looked in the direction in which Loppy was pointing and saw a great wall of water, like a tidal wave, cascading down toward them through the opening in the hills!

Chapter 11

Incorrigible River

he four watched the approach of the river with feelings of awe. Whistle Stick was so thunderstruck that he could not even grumble. The great waves were tremendous and terrible. They came foaming and bubbling and rolling in mighty billows down the valley. Finally, they were swirling about the foot of the very hill where Ruth Ann and her friends stood.

"O . . . ooh!" gasped the girl. "What if the river doesn't stop, but comes right up over this hill?"

The others answered her with a shiver, but Loppy Wallops quickly explained, "It's simply impossible to tell what he'll do! He's perfectly incorrigible, that river."

Indeed, for a time it did seem that they were in deadly peril. The river continued to rise until all the smaller hills were completely out of sight and only the summit of the peak that held Ruth Ann and her companions stood up out of the foaming water.

Then quite suddenly, all the foaming and the swirling stopped, and the four frightened spectators heard the jolliest laugh come bubbling up to them from the waters at their feet. They looked down, and there, outlined in tiny ripples, was as round and cheery a face as anyone had ever seen!

One sight of that laughing countenance, however, and Loppy Wallops started for Incorrigible River with his cudgel.

Lifting the heavy stick high in his right hand, he advanced shouting, "What's the meaning of all this fuss and commotion? Don't you know any better than to go around swamping the country? Get back to your source where you belong!" The little man struck at the river furiously with his club.

Incorrigible River only laughed and laughed!

"You're always hitting me for something that isn't my fault," he gurgled. "I'm not to blame when I swell up and overflow my banks. You mustn't mind his harsh words," he continued, looking at Ruth Ann. "Loppy Wallops is really a good fellow and is only doing his duty when he tries to whip me into shape. What he doesn't understand is that I can't help being incorrigible. If I could help it, I would. It isn't any fun boiling up higher and higher and leaving my comfortable home for a strange valley and strange hills. You know that, don't you?"

"Well, whatever makes you do it, then?" questioned Ruth Ann, whose eyes were wide with these extraordinary happenings.

"It's this way," laughed River. "There'll be a time when I'll be perfectly respectable and have a jolly time rolling back and forth in little waves about the source that is my home. Then all of a sudden, Black Weeper will begin to cry, and it's all over as far as my trying to be good is concerned. The more Black Weeper cries, the worse I get. I foam and sputter, and my nice little ripples get wider and wider and fiercer and fiercer, until I have to leave my home and Sighing Cavern altogether and burst out all over the valley, in the terrifying style that you have just witnessed."

The tale of Incorrigible River left Loppy Wallops unconvinced however.

"He's telling some such tale excusing himself," remarked the Guardian of the River. "What he needs is a good licking!" And again he advanced on the jolly river with his great cudgel upraised.

Ruth Ann stepped in front of him immediately! "My mother says, 'Never whip a naughty child. You may find that he has a *real* excuse for being naughty.' Perhaps Incorrigible River is telling the truth. Perhaps it is Black Weeper that makes him overflow!"

"Who is this Black Weeper?" broke in Whistle Stick, who had been listening attentively to the conversation.

"That," gurgled River, "I can't tell you."

"There, you see!" exclaimed Loppy Wallops, triumphantly. "It's all a fish story, every bit of it, just as I told you!"

"Well, I believe what River says." Here Lonesome came to the rescue. "I know just how he feels out here among all these strange hills and valleys. I tell you, he's mighty brave to keep on laughing so far away from his home. I know what it means to be all alone in an unknown country," and Lonesome sniffed reminiscently.

"Many thanks!" laughed Incorrigible River. "I know it does sound bad when I blame Black Weeper for my naughtiness and then can't even explain who Black Weeper is. But to tell you the truth, I've never seen the face of Black Weeper, at all. It's covered with a long black veil!"

"O . . . ooh, doesn't that sound mysterious!" cried Ruth Ann. "How I wish we might see him—or is it her?"

"You can't get that answer from me," River bubbled, "but perhaps we could fix it up so that you could all see it—you've treated me swell, all of you, even Loppy Wallops here, who's only done what he thought was his duty." The river laughed happily again.

At this suggestion, Whistle Stick shook his head.

"What's the use of putting ourselves into more danger all the time? Here at least we're safe for a moment, and I don't mind telling you that this weird country is too full of the Enemy Birds, Incorrigible River, and such things to suit me!"

"Poor old dear," said Ruth Ann, putting her arm about the old fellow's neck. "You'll come, anyway, won't you, just to please me? You know that you and Lonesome and I promised to stay together."

"Well," he grumbled, trying not to show how really pleased he was at her concern, "if you put it that way, I suppose I'll have to go."

"But how will we ever get to the Black Weeper?" asked Ruth Ann. "We haven't the sign of a boat."

At this, even Incorrigible River looked a bit worried.

"That's so, and without a boat it's quite impossible to travel to my source, where Black Weeper is."

"This might do for a sail," offered the snake, as he produced his cherished possession, the prized bandana. "It's quite large and made of stout material. I could stand perfectly straight and hold it out—like this."

Suiting the action to his words, Lonesome held out the handkerchief. The wind caught it and bellowed it out until it made a respectable sail. Indeed, the force of the wind caught between its four corners was so great that it took Snake off his feet and he landed 'smack-dab' on Whistle Stick's tender feet.

"Ouch! Mind where you blow!" growled Stick. "You're making a fool of yourself!"

"Is that so?" retorted the snake. "I was at least offering to help, which is more than I've heard from you!"

"Well it's not as if I can't help," answered Whistle Stick, slyly. "I could help more than anybody—if I'd a mind to."

"He's right. He's right!" cried Ruth Ann. "He's wood! Wood floats! Oh, he'd make a wonderful boat for us!"

At Ruth Ann's words, Whistle Stick swelled all up with his own importance and gazed victoriously at Lonesome as much as to say: "There now, see what I told you?"

"Whistle Stick, please be our boat," begged the girl. "You can turn your face up and keep it out of the water. It will be such a wonderful adventure to visit Black Weeper and see the source of Incorrigible River."

"I think you've all gone crazy!" Whistle Stick announced. "I can't see why you aren't content to stay here. But there's no fun in being safe all alone, so I guess I'll have to go on your fool's chase with you."

Ruth Ann clapped her hands. "I knew he'd help! Let's get ready for the cruise. Here, Whistle Stick, if you'll just lie down face up on the river, I'll hold you to the hill until we're ready to start sailing."

Still grumbling to himself over their foolishness, the stick did as the girl requested. He could not repress a bit of a shiver as he slid into the water. Ruth Ann held his hand tight to moor him to the hill, while Lonesome climbed out and took his position with the bandana, as a mast and sail. The girl turned to Loppy Wallops who had watched the preparations for departure with the keenest interest.

"You're coming too, of course?" she asked the Guardian of the River politely.

Loppy Wallops shook his head.

"No, I can't," he answered. "You see, I have to stay on the outside of Sighing Cavern even when Incorrigible River recedes to the source, so that I can be ready for his next overflow. If I got inside Sighing Cavern and River started on one of his naughty spells, there wouldn't be any way for me to beat him to the outside country, and he might do even more damage than usual. I'll just wait here, thank you! When you have all disappeared into Sighing Cavern and the floor of the country is drying, I'll walk back and take up my customary position at the entrance to the cavern."

"I'm sorry that you feel that you mustn't come with us," said Ruth Ann courteously, "but if you feel it is your duty not to accompany us, why of course you can't."

So saying, she shook hands gravely with the little Pinhead and sat down at the stern of the strange craft, right over Whistle Stick's feet.

Just as Lonesome was about to hold out his bandana sail, Ruth Ann thought of something she had forgotten.

"Wait!" she cried. "Wait! Before we start out, we must have a rudder to guide us! Every boat must have a rudder!"

They all looked about anxiously for a moment. Then Loppy Wallops had a thought.

"Here," he said. "I haven't helped at all. This cudgel is mighty valuable to me—but you take it. It will do for a rudder!"

"Thank you, so much!" breathed Ruth Ann, gratefully.

"Remember, you," warned Loppy, turning his attention to Incorrigible River, "if anything happens to these friends of mine while they're in your care, I'll find that club sooner or later and give you the worst walloping you ever had!"

River only laughed at the threat. And so the strange boat with its odd little crew started out, with Ruth Ann holding the Pinhead's cudgel behind her for a rudder and taking her directions from Incorrigible River, who gurgled happily along behind them.

Chapter 12

Grotto of Sighing Snails

 lowly the company of three sailed toward the opening in the hills from where Incorrigible River had come bursting forth upon the valley in mighty waves.

If it had not been for the uncomfortable positions that Whistle Stick and Lonesome Snake were forced to keep up, Ruth Ann would have been delighted with the trip. River was on his best behavior and only little ripples marred his smooth surface. He was following his new friends, bubbling and gurgling with laughter just behind Loppy Wallops's club.

Everything in High Country seemed perfectly peaceful. A soft glow of light still pervaded the land. The quiet motion of the boat and the lapping of water against Whistle Stick were like a lullaby.

On and on they glided, over the still waters, until they neared the opening in the hill from where the flood had started.

Only then was Ruth Ann able to make out what had not been apparent before. Cut through between the rows of hills was a low black tunnel. A low-swung arch hung over its entrance and within its depths. It looked terrifyingly dark and mysterious.

"That," said Incorrigible River, "is the entrance to Sighing Cavern, the location of my source."

"Goodness me! Isn't its arch hung low!" cried the girl. "I don't believe we'll ever be able to get under it."

"Duck low!" she cried to Lonesome. "Duck low as ever you can, or the arch will knock you off into the water! Look out, everybody!"

As she screamed her warning, the boat swished around one side of the low tunnel and swept inside on the current of Incorrigible River, who was now receding rapidly.

Once inside the gloomy recess, none of the friends could see a thing. Coming into complete darkness from the glow of the outside country was such a change that the black of the tunnel seemed impenetrable. Ruth Ann could not help shuddering, while Whistle Stick groaned aloud.

"It does seem as if this adventure is a trifle more than we bargained for," said Lonesome to Ruth Ann, in a half whisper. He was lying flattened out on Whistle Stick with his face very near the girl's. Ruth Ann was bending low to escape the danger from the roof of the arch that narrowly missed the top of her head as they were swept along.

"I can't see my hand before my face, can you?" asked the snake.

"No, I can't," whispered Ruth Ann in an awed tone. "What do you suppose is going to become of us?"

Incorrigible River, all but forgotten by the little crew, gave forth a laugh which was a comforting sort of thing in that dismal place.

"Never fear," he gurgled, still close behind them. "Soon we'll be in safer waters. Keep up your courage! Here we go! I never seem to be able to keep myself in control in this channel because I recede so fast. Please sit tight and don't worry!"

As River finished speaking, the full strength of the retreating current struck poor old Whistle Stick and started him on a mad flight down the narrow dark tunnel. Faster and faster ran the tide, and swifter and swifter went Whistle Stick. Once, the waters foamed up over his mouth and nose and he coughed and spit and almost capsized Ruth Ann and Lonesome.

Ruth Ann had long since been obliged to give up all attempts at guiding her strange craft. All that she could do was stretch out low beside Lonesome and hold on tight to Whistle Stick, to keep from being thrown off into the rushing water. Making the positions of the snake and Ruth Ann still more dangerous, their little boat had to keep wiggling constantly about in order to keep his nose and mouth above water. Innumerable times the passengers felt sure that the next moment the waters of the river would close over them.

Suddenly, all the rushing noises ceased and the three travelers took such a drop through space that it took Ruth Ann's breath away. Both Lonesome and Whistle Stick gasped with the surprise of it!

At first, Ruth Ann kept her eyes shut tight, afraid of what she might see if she opened them. Finally, as nothing happened, she could again feel the quiet rocking motion of Whistle Stick just as it had felt outside the channel on calm waters. She opened one eye a bit, and then, as she took in the strangeness of her new surroundings, the other eye popped open of its own accord.

"O . . . ooh!" She prodded Lonesome with a finger. "Do sit up and look. Isn't this the strangest place you ever saw in your life?"

Fearfully, Lonesome uncoiled himself and sat up to look about too.

"Dearie me! Dearie me! What have we gotten into?"

Whistle Stick, feeling safe for the moment, was his own grumbling self again.

"Well," said he, "I hope you're satisfied at last! We'll never be able to get out of this place. We've had such a dreadful time getting in. Besides, in the position I'm in, I can't see anything but the top of the cavern, and it looks like a most uninteresting top."

"At least we've stopped rushing along at that frightful rate," comforted Ruth Ann. "That's something to be thankful for!"

They were now drifting in quite a large pool. There was a faint light, like Earth's twilight, illuminating the walls of the dark grotto in which they found themselves. Huge pieces of rock hung down from the roof overhead like fantastic icicles. Low sounds like myriad sighs came constantly from all about them. It was a weird place, surely.

"Well, folks," came a cheery gurgle from behind Whistle Stick. "You beat me in. It always takes some running for me to keep up with my current in the channel. But now we're all here together again. How do you like it?"

"Terrible, what I can see of it," groaned Whistle Stick, as he grunted and twisted in an effort to ease his cramped position. "It'll take me the rest of my life to get all the water out of my joints."

"Where in the world are we?" asked Ruth Ann. "This is the most curious place I've ever seen."

"This grotto," bubbled Incorrigible River, "is called the Grotto of Sighing Snails."

"Sighing Snails!" Ruth Ann was awestruck.

"Yes," answered River. "The walls and the roof of the grotto are covered with them. They're the things that are making those pitiful little noises that you hear coming from every direction."

"I catch snails on Earth sometimes for my mother at a cent apiece," explained Ruth Ann. "They eat our roses and vines. They're awful pests, but I have never heard of snails sighing before! Can we get close enough to see them?"

"Yes," replied River, "but you'll have to paddle with Loppy Wallops's cudgel, because by the time I get to the grotto I'm so exhausted that I can't possibly help anyone at all."

The girl took Loppy's club and paddled slowly, until Whistle Stick lay quite close to a wall of the grotto. There she could see the snails quite clearly, hundreds and thousands of them, large snails, small snails, firmly fastened to the grotto walls. They were even clinging to the rock icicles that hung from the roof overhead. All of the snails, little and big, sighed regularly and pathetically, all of them together.

"It's really too sad for words," sympathized Lonesome, wiping his eyes on the red bandana. "My heart always goes out to anything in sorrow."

"Listen to it!" growled Whistle Stick. "His heart! Doesn't that just make you sick? Everybody in the world knows the size of a snake's heart."

Ruth Ann was too interested and excited over the Sighing Snails to be concerned with this new controversy between her friends. Besides, she was getting rather used to their silly bickering.

"Do you suppose that they speak?" she asked eagerly, turning to Incorrigible River.

"I'm sure I don't know!" he bubbled in his jolly voice. "I've never taken the trouble to ask them. But you might try. Pick out a big one though, for I've an idea that a little one, if it speaks at all, would speak much too softly for you to hear it."

"Very well." Summoning her courage Ruth Ann leaned over toward the wall and picked out a large over-grown snail with a fat sigh.

"Excuse me, please," said she, in her most polite manner. "But can you speak?"

"Indeed, and why not?" came the indignant answer from the snail. "I've got a mouth and a vocal box, and that's all anyone needs if one is to talk. If I didn't have speaking apparatus in my throat, how could I sigh?"

"I'm sure I don't know," replied Ruth Ann, taken aback by the suddenness of the snail's retort. "The snails that I'm used to on Earth never made any sort of a noise that I could hear, and they're very slow crawlers. They take ages to go anywhere."

"Stupid creatures!" stated the snail, abruptly. "What do they want to go anywhere for? What's the use of crawling about if one can stay right still and sigh for a living?"

"Sigh for a living!" repeated Ruth Ann, surprised. "That sounds as if you were paid for sighing."

"And so we are," assented the snail. "It's a trade with us!"

"It's their *line*—sighing!" said Ruth Ann, directing a serious whisper toward Whistle Stick. "We must remember to tell the Green Blowster!"

"But if you're paid for sighing, someone must pay you," put in Lonesome, addressing the snail.

"We're all in the employ of Black Weeper," answered the snail with dignity. "Black Weeper is a true artist and we supply the proper surroundings for him. You see, he can weep so much better in a sad place that he hires us to make him feel sorrow all around him. He is a wonderful weeper, the most perfect weeper in the world," added the snail with a bit of envy creeping into its voice.

"Weeping must be Black Weeper's ***line***, then," explained Ruth Ann in another aside to Whistle Stick.

"He sounds like a very sensible sort," he answered. "That's what I call a useful occupation—weeping. I only wish I knew how, but I guess I haven't been alive long enough to learn," he added, trying his best to see the snail, and almost tipping off Ruth Ann and Lonesome in his attempt.

"Keep on the way you've started and you'll soon have the art of weeping mastered," Lonesome snapped in disgust. "Of all the calamity howlers . . ."

Ignoring her silly quarrelsome friends, Ruth Ann inquired eagerly of the large snail, "Where shall we find Black Weeper?"

She was all on fire to see this mysterious weeper of whom the snail spoke so highly.

"Go straight ahead and then around," answered the snail with a heavy sigh. "Goodbye and good luck."

"Don't forget you'll have to paddle," came the jolly warning of River.

"I won't," said the girl.

Taking up Loppy Wallops's cudgel for a paddle, Ruth Ann began to propel Whistle Stick out into the center of the grotto and onward in her search for Black Weeper.

Chapter 13

Black Weeper

lowly the strange craft and its passengers made their way across the grotto to a bend in the subterranean cavern. There through a low, wide arch, our friends beheld another pool, smaller than the one in which they were.

In the new cavern, the water was absolutely still; not a ripple broke its surface. From the far end came a steady 'drip, drip, drip.' There, dimly outlined in the semi-darkness, stood a great dark form!

One look at the ghostly shape and Ruth Ann's heart jumped with something very much like fright.

"Are you sure that no harm will come to us?" she whispered to the jolly river. "You see, I feel very responsible for Lonesome and Whistle Stick. They're my friends and they would not be here, at all, if it were not for me."

"I've never known Black Weeper to injure anything," Incorrigible River assured her. "It's too busy weeping."

Ruth Ann and the Green Blowster

"Shall we paddle right up close to it?" asked Ruth Ann of her friends.

"Go as far as you like," groaned Stick. "Personally, Black Weeper is the one thing about this terrible country for which I have the slightest sympathy."

"Certainly, go right up to it," agreed the snake. "We probably couldn't get away from it anyway if it wanted to hurt us."

The girl took a firmer grasp on her paddle and propelled the boat slowly toward the tall, terrifying, black shape of the weeper.

As they drew near the gigantic form, it assumed definite lines and Ruth Ann realized that she was indeed looking at the very source of Incorrigible River. On a jutting promontory stood Black Weeper. Its great shape was covered from head to toe with clouds of gossamer black that shook gently, as piteous sobs emerged from the dark depths.

Try as she could, Ruth Ann was unable to distinguish a single feature of Black Weeper's face. The only parts of its body that were in plain view were two great hands, wrinkled with age, that held suspended in front of it a low earthen bowl.

It was into this bowl that tears were falling and causing the gentle drip, drip, drip that had first caught the ears of the friends as they ventured into this cavern. The bowl was now full and running over into the pool itself.

From the grotto came the low, piteous sighs of the snails, in tune with the sobs of the weeper and the regular drip, drip,

drip of its tears. The sounds all combined to create an impression of the deepest melancholy, causing Ruth Ann herself to shiver as with a chill.

Nevertheless, she was determined to find out what it was all about. She paddled yet a bit closer to the terrifying weeper and spoke to it in a voice that she tried her best to keep steady, but that trembled in spite of her.

"Mr . . . Mr. Weeper?"

Black Weeper was just too busy with its weeping to hear her. It made not a move under its black veils, nor did the huge hands that held the earthenware bowl shake the least bit with surprise at the unexpected visitors.

"Try again—louder," urged Incorrigible River. "I've always wanted to know myself what the old fellow wept about."

Clearing her throat, "Ahh-huuummm," Ruth Ann addressed Black Weeper again, but with much firmer and clearer tones this time.

"Beg pardon, sir, but will you answer a few questions for us?"

As her voice ceased, a tremble passed over the giant figure, and a sob, heavier than any before, came forth from the depth of its dark robes.

"Replying to questions is not my *line*," answered a deep, mournful voice from behind the veils. "I'm a professional weeper. However, if you'll ask your questions, I'll see whether or not I can answer them."

"First then," said Ruth Ann, taking heart from the great

weeper's mournful but kindly voice, "why do you weep so?"

"I *weep*," replied the black figure with a sniffle, "because it is my business to weep. It's the thing I do best . . . it is my **line**. I can weep regularly and with enthusiasm."

"But what," continued Ruth Ann, "is there for you to weep about?"

"Now that's what I call a foolish question," fussed Whistle Stick, impatiently. "I could answer that one myself. There's plenty to weep about, goodness knows!"

"Keep still, will you!" rebuked Lonesome. "It's Black Weeper that we're interested in at present, not you and your troubles."

"*What* I weep about," came in the slow, mournful tones of Black Weeper, "I consider is none of my business. I weep because I am paid to weep. For ages, I have been the Official Weeper for the entire Pinhead People."

"Pinhead People!" repeated Ruth Ann, amazed. "Why we know one of them—Loppy Wallops, Guardian of Incorrigible River."

"Indeed!" Black Weeper expressed its surprise politely, but sadly. "I'm not acquainted with any of them myself."

"But surely if you work for them," continued Ruth Ann, who could not help showing her astonishment, "you must know some of them!"

"No, I do not," reaffirmed Black Weeper, pausing an instant to sob and shed two tears. "If *they* set me here on these rocks, it was so long ago that I've forgotten all about it."

"Why, how strange," persisted Ruth Ann. "Then you've been here for years and years, haven't you?"

"I haven't the slightest idea what a year is," answered Black Weeper mournfully, "but I can't ever remember being anywhere else."

Lonesome, who had become confused by this puzzlement, wondered aloud, "If the Pinheads pay you for weeping, you must see the one who pays you your salary . . . ."

"No, I have never seen any of the Pinheads."

"Now," it continued, "do you see that large flat rock immediately behind my head?"

When the listeners nodded assent, Black Weeper went on with its explanation. "Every so often, a Pinhead opens that rock window by simply removing the rock. I never look around because I want every Pinhead to feel that I'm always on the job; I just continue weeping. Pinhead Deputy Stepit, who brings me my salary, shoves it through the opening made by the removal of the rock, gives me instructions regarding future weepings, and then replaces the rock. You see if the Pinhead people are happy, I do not have to weep so bitterly and so constantly as I must when sadness is abroad in the land. By nature, the Pinheads are a very happy people. They hate to weep. That's why they hired me in the first place, to do the weeping for the entire country!"

"Do they pay you with gold pieces?" inquired Lonesome.

"No," replied Black Weeper, sorrowfully, "they pay me with goldfish eggs."

"Goldfish eggs!" exclaimed Ruth Ann. "How absurd!"

"Yes, isn't it?"

"What possible use have you for goldfish eggs?"

"None whatever. That's why they pay me with them. It really disappoints me to be paid with something that I can't use, so I weep just that much better."

"These Pinheads appeal to me," muttered Whistle Stick to himself. "They must be very special people."

"Of course," explained Black Weeper, "there is one use that I've discovered for the goldfish eggs. I hand them over to my snails!"

"But snails don't eat fish eggs, do they?" asked Ruth Ann. "I know that the snails of Earth have no use for anything of the sort."

"Oh no," agreed the weeper, "my snails have nothing whatsoever that they can do with the eggs. It serves to make them even more unhappy so that their sighs are more and more heart wrenching after each time I pay them!"

"Do the Pinheads settle with you regularly?" questioned Whistle Stick. "It must be wonderful to be able to make a business of being sad. Everybody is always pouncing on me for my grumbling."

"No, my salary isn't paid to me regularly," explained Black Weeper. "You see, I get one goldfish egg a tear and usually the

Pinheads owe me for about 43,200 tears before they pay me my due. Occasionally, when an unusual time of affliction hits the country, and it's very, very difficult for the Pinheads to stay happy, they pay me one million goldfish eggs in advance."

"That makes me remember," added Black Weeper, "there must be some terrible happening going on right now in Pinhead Country, for they've paid me two sacks of goldfish eggs in advance, and I've been weeping steadily now for a long time. That's what's been the matter with Incorrigible River. He just has to rise up and overflow his banks when I get one of my bad weeping spells!"

"Hear! Hear!" gurgled River. "What did I tell you? I hope you folks will explain to Loppy, if you ever see him again, what Black Weeper has just told you. I knew it wasn't my fault when I swelled up and swamped the country!"

"Whatever can be the matter with the Pinheads that they are so unhappy lately?" puzzled Ruth Ann anxiously.

Her tender heart ached for anyone in trouble. She was certain that some frightful disaster must have befallen the happy Pinheads to make them pay Black Weeper to weep for them so hard and so ceaselessly.

"That, as I told you at first, is no concern of mine. I weep well and I weep according to my instructions. That is all that matters to me."

Just at this point in the conversation, a hollow thud broke upon the ears of the little party at the source. As the thud reverberated throughout the recesses of the cavern, the Sighing

Snails quieted and even Black Weeper stopped sobbing tears for a moment.

"That," the weeper explained, in tones as near to excitement as it had shown, "that is Deputy Pinhead Stepit with another sack of goldfish eggs! Make haste and hide yourselves, strange beings, before he sees you. If he finds that I have been talking instead of weeping, he may cut my wages!"

Hurriedly Ruth Ann complied with Black Weeper's request. Grasping the paddle once more, she drove Whistle Stick rapidly along the promontory of jutting rock, and clambering onto it quickly, she pulled Lonesome and Whistle Stick up beside her. The three friends then leaned far back against the cavern wall in order to be out of sight of Deputy Pinhead as he paid Black Weeper.

Slowly, the great flat rock was lifted out of the wall and a hand appeared in the opening. In the hand was a large sack that it deposited on the floor immediately behind Black Weeper, who was industriously sobbing and weeping again.

"Weep, Black One, Official Weeper of the Pinheads," cried a high shrill voice. "Weep as you have never wept before. Terrible is the affliction that has befallen our happy people, and difficult indeed it is for the Pinheads to be joyful even with the greatest weeper of all shedding its tears for them!"

So saying, the voice died away and the great rock came back to rest in its place as part of the cavern wall.

Ruth Ann and the Green Blowster

Chapter 14

Through the Rock Window

o sooner had the enormous rock fallen into its place than Ruth Ann ran eagerly to the place where the opening had been. Following cautiously behind were Whistle Stick and Lonesome Snake.

"I'll tell you what . . ." she began.

But Whistle Stick, who was walking with joints stiff from his long period in the river, stopped her.

"Don't say it! Don't say it!" he groaned. "I know what you want to do. You want to go into the Land of the Pinheads and try to help them out of their troubles, but I've had just all of this I can stand!"

"Try to brace up and be a bit of a man, anyway," objected Lonesome Snake. "The Pinheads have the reputation of being a jolly people, not dangerous. That's certainly to their credit!"

"Do you suppose that we could climb through that rock window?" called Ruth Ann to Black Weeper, pointing at the flat stone in the wall through which the mysterious hand had pushed the sack of goldfish eggs.

But Black Weeper, who had unmistakably regretted his short vacation from work, was now more busily sobbing and weeping than ever and answered never a word.

The Incorrigible River, however, who had followed our friends into hiding and out again to the rock window, cocked his head to one side examining the flat rock attentively for a moment.

"I believe the three of you, by working together, could push that stone through the opening," he gurgled finally. "Then you could all climb through and into the Pinhead Country!"

"You're the most satisfactory river," cried Ruth Ann happily. "I'd give you a big hug if you weren't so *wet*!"

"If he weren't so wet? The three of us get into trouble enough without any help from an outsider!" groused Whistle Stick.

Ruth Ann, never-minding the grumpy fellow, had made up her mind to continue into Pinhead territory. She was not going to let a few grumbles from Whistle Stick stand in the way.

"Oh, Whistle Stick," she pleaded, "please remember your promise to keep with us in our adventures! We may really be able to help the Pinheads—and besides," here her voice sank to an excited whisper, "we may find Dukey Daddles on the other side of that rock wall!"

"Dogs never meant that much in my life," muttered Whistle Stick, "and they're meaning less and less every minute!"

Lonesome, who had been studying the flat rock, broke into their conversation.

"Let's get started. If Ruth Ann will stand in the center and let Stick and me stand on each side, and we all push together, we'll have no trouble moving the rock, I'm sure! If you will notice, it trembles at the slightest shove."

For proof of this, Lonesome gave the flat stone a slight push and it tottered back and forth a bit on its foundation.

"Whistle Stick, it's going to be easy," and without more ado the excited little girl pushed the protesting wooden man to her right side. Lonesome was already at her left.

"Now, when I count three, let's all shove on the rock as hard as we can. One . . . two . . . three!"

As the final number left her lips, the three exerted their utmost effort. The rock wobbled back and forth and at last, with a lurch, dropped through the opening into the outside country!

"Now that's done!" exclaimed Ruth Ann joyfully. "All that remains for us to do is to get up and out of the opening and into Pinhead Country. Come, Whistle Stick, I'll help you through first because you're lighter than Lonesome."

Ruth Ann and the Green Blowster

"Not much, you won't," he protested. "I'm not a bit anxious to be the first out into that perilous country!"

"Here," said the snake, "push me over. If there are any hostile folks out there, they may not know about my tail and think that I'm dangerous. I'm not afraid."

"All right," agreed Ruth Ann. "Over you go!" And stooping down to lift up the tip of Lonesome's tail, she hoisted him up and over the aperture until, with a lunge and a wiggle, he vanished from sight.

"Now I'll have to put you over," she said, turning to Whistle Stick. "You're still so stiff that I'm afraid you'd never get over the wall by yourself. You'd have to stay in here, all alone!"

"That," grumbled Whistle Stick under his breath, "wouldn't worry me much!"

In spite of his protesting, he let Ruth Ann help him through the rock window. Then with a merry goodbye and a wave of her hand to Black Weeper and Incorrigible River, she caught hold of the rock at the base of the window. With a little jump and a mighty tug, she threw her weight through the opening and landed with a soft thud beside her two friends in the Country of the Pinheads!

They found themselves on the summit of a hill looking down upon a strange and not unbeautiful sight. Again the soft glow of light that they had noticed at first in High Country pervaded the scene. As far as they could see, the ground was carpeted with a deep green. There were no trees, but here and there grew a single bush or clump of bushes, some of them much higher than Ruth Ann's head, and all of them with bright green leaves of exactly the same shade.

Far down below, in the valley, were a number of brightly colored little houses. One of them was a turreted building, probably the town hall. It stood near the shores of a tiny lake that glimmered in the light, as if its waters were crystal clear.

Suddenly Ruth Ann, whose eyes had come back to rest on the green at her feet, bent over with a startled exclamation. Then she stooped to feel the greensward at her feet.

"Why of all the marvels," she cried. "Guess what this is? I thought it was close cut grass; but it's nothing but green felt!"

Running across to a clump of the brilliant bushes, she eagerly felt the leaves and branches.

"And these—oh, Whistle Stick, Lonesome, whatever do you think? These bright green leaves are all cut out of shiny calico! And the twigs . . . and the stalks . . . why they're nothing but thin wire, wrapped round and round with brown tissue paper!"

"It's an imitation country," said Lonesome. "There's nothing real about it. What a terrible place to be homesick for!"

"We're apt to find out that it's all imitation but the danger," muttered Whistle Stick. "The danger will probably be real enough!"

Even as he spoke, Ruth Ann's sharp eyes had made out some tiny figures below them, far down the hill. Evidently, they were keeping to a path worn to the distant village from the very place where Ruth Ann and her friends stood. The little figures were walking with military precision and seemed to be carrying muskets over their shoulders.

It was Whistle Stick who offered the first explanation.

"Why, it's Deputy Pinhead and his bodyguards," he said, "going home after presenting Black Weeper with his advance salary."

"For once, you've said something that makes sense," agreed the snake.

"Of course that's who they are," cried Ruth Ann.

"Let's follow down the path and see where they go," suggested Lonesome.

Whistle Stick's only answer was a groan of reluctance.

Before the trio could act upon any suggestion, however, a terrible thing happened!

The great flat rock, that the friends had pushed out of the wall of Dark Cavern and had balanced on the crown of the hill beside them, suddenly became dislodged and started rolling and thundering down the hill, gaining momentum as it went. It roared straight down the little path, careening down the incline to the little village in the distance.

The three who watched it from the top of the hill were

not the only ones who were aware of the great stone in its downward flight.

No sooner had the rock started than the Deputy and his band heard it coming down toward them from above. The Pinhead official and his men faced about and ran nimbly out of the way of the huge stone as it plunged past them.

When the danger from it was over, the men stood, faces to the crest of the hill, and began to gesticulate frantically in the direction of Ruth Ann and her companions. Obviously, the Pinheads had sighted our adventurers and were wondering excitedly *who* they were and *what* to do about them.

"There now, what did I tell you?" ventured Whistle Stick. "Ten to one, they'll decide to come back here and get us. Goodness only knows what fate will have in store for us then."

"Perhaps we can climb back into Sighing Cavern," suggested the snake, who was getting a bit uneasy himself.

One look at the rock wall behind them, and the trio was forced to give up any idea of escape in that direction. The distance from the ground to the rock window was much greater on the Pinhead side of the wall than it was on the side of Black Weeper. It would be impossible for Ruth Ann, try as she might, to shove Lonesome and Whistle Stick up into the opening, let alone clamber into it herself.

They were forced to wait for the decision of the Pinheads, which was not long in coming. After a moment or two of excited conferring, their band charged back up the hill with Deputy Pinhead in advance of his group that numbered six members.

"The majority is certainly with them," said the stick fellow. "They have the advantage of numbers, all right."

"Do you suppose that it would do any good for me to disguise my tail with my bandana and try to fool them the way I did the Enemy Birds?" asked Lonesome, in a hurried whisper.

"No, I don't" replied Ruth Ann, frankly. "I don't believe that they've ever seen any kind of snake. We'll just have to wait and take a chance that they'll not harm us."

"A good chance that is, too," moaned Whistle Stick. "They don't seem to be in a sweet and gentle mood from where I stand!"

Indeed, the behavior of the little band was far from comforting to the watchers on the hill. For as they charged up the slope, the Deputy was waving his weapon aloft in a very warlike attitude. The others followed his example by waving their arms above their heads and shouting as they ran.

All the men were dressed like Loppy Wallops in bright red coats, green pants, and polished brass buttons. At first, Ruth Ann thought that the weapons that they carried over their shoulders were guns, but as soon as the men drew near, she found out to her distress that they were carrying hard rubber hammers!

These hammers the Pinheads used expertly. Long before they came up to the trio, Ruth Ann and her friends had felt the sharp stinging blows of the little men's weapons. For the hammer heads were fastened upon long lengths of stout elastic tape that allowed the Pinheads to hurl them at their victims and then draw them back quickly for another shot.

The blows from the rubber hammer heads did hurt, but Ruth Ann and her friends had resolved to be brave. Not a tear did they show as the cruel little Deputy and his band surrounded them.

Deputy Pinhead was the spokesman.

"I arrest you in the name of Her Majesty, the Queen!" he pronounced in his shrill voice. "Strangers in Pinhead Country are never welcome, and at present, you are even less welcome than usual. We are in the throes of a plague and we have no time for hospitality. We've plenty of trouble of our own without the trouble of entertaining visitors. I shall advise Her Majesty to dispose of you at once."

"I don't like the way he said that," Whistle Stick whispered to Ruth Ann. "It sounded as if he meant it!"

"Let's not show them that we're frightened, anyway," she whispered back. "Remember, we all three came from Earth where they have great soldiers! Let's look them straight in the eyes!"

So saying, Ruth Ann drew herself up to her full height and addressed Deputy Pinhead.

"We are harmless travelers," she declared, "and we do not understand why we should be treated in this rude manner. We are looking through High Country for my dog, Dukey Daddles, who was run into heaven by a truck."

"We do not know anything at all about 'dogs' as you call them," responded the Deputy.

"You don't know much about anything, do you?" muttered Whistle Stick, under his breath.

"What's that?" asked Deputy Pinhead sharply.

"Try to find out!" responded the stick sulkily before subsiding into absolute silence.

The Deputy glared at Whistle Stick suspiciously, but went on. "Whether you are harmless or not, does not matter. The truth of it is that a plague, such as the happy Pinheads have never known, has descended upon us and we trust no one!"

"A plague?" said Ruth Ann. "What kind of plague?"

Evidently the affair was too horrible even to discuss, for at Ruth Ann's query, the little Deputy turned white and answered her not a word.

Instead, he faced his men with a military order. "Surround and bind them!"

After securing their captives, the Pinheads took their positions, two ahead of the prisoners, one on each side of them, and two in the rear.

Deputy Stepit took his place in front of the procession and commanded, "Shoulder arms!"

At this, the rubber hammers were carried to the shoulders of all the soldiers.

"Forward! March!"

The company set off at a brisk rate down the path toward the tiny village, with the lake gleaming like a diamond in the glow.

Chapter 15

Audience with the Queen of the Pinheads

s the Deputy and his prisoners drew near the outskirts of the town, an amazing fact became apparent to the three friends.

"How extraordinary!" exclaimed Lonesome.

"Why, I declare," cried Ruth Ann, "the houses are made out of children's building blocks!"

"Why?" asked Whistle Stick, whose surprise was genuine and had taken lead over his grumbling for the time being.

"Why what?" inquired Deputy Stepit at whom Whistle Stick had aimed his question.

"Why do you have houses made of building blocks?"

"Why not?" said the Deputy, gruffly. At which Whistle Stick's grumpiness returned and he subsided again into disinterested silence.

As the little company filed into the village, news of the strangers was carried from house to house, and groups of

Pinheads rushed out of homes and offices to assemble on the street corners to see them pass.

Judging from the mutterings and veiled threats that were flung at Ruth Ann and her fellow prisoners, the trio could not expect much mercy at the hands of the Pinheads.

In spite of the danger, Ruth Ann gazed at the peculiar dwellings with keen interest. They were made of every sort of building block imaginable, and the blocks had been set up in every conceivable way. Some of them were colored in plain shades, some had pictures from fairy tales printed on them, some bore raised letters of the alphabet, and some were just plain wood, untinted. The houses themselves ranged in architecture from simple square structures to rather large two-storied buildings with arches and porticoes. All the houses had one feature in common. They had no windows and only one door, usually a large one in front of the building.

The little company passed quickly down one street and up another, until suddenly Deputy Stepit cried:

"Halt!"

They were immediately in front of a great arch that led over a path of inlaid diamond-shaped blocks set in the felt greensward to a great door in the most pretentious building in the village. It was the one with turrets that the adventurers had sighted with their first glimpse of the town.

The building was made of blocks of all shapes and hues and rose five stories high, finished at the top with towers and turrets like a miniature castle. The Deputy advanced alone along the path and entered the door, leaving his men to look after the prisoners.

Their wait was short. Almost immediately, two Pinheads with long tin whistles appeared at the entrance to the building. They blew one note on their whistles, in shrill unison. Then Deputy Stepit appeared in the door and waved them to enter.

"I never did like tin whistles; wood makes a much better tone," remarked Whistle Stick with a superior air.

"That whistle's for us! Get a move on, you!" said one of the guards as he prodded Stick in the back with his hard rubber hammer.

"Here's where I give up all hope," bemoaned the stick as he started along the path.

"You never had any hope in you to give up," retorted Lonesome.

"Once inside that place, we're doomed," continued Whistle Stick, ignoring the snake's remark. "It looks like a jail!"

Down the path and through the great doorway went the strange band and there were halted again by the two Pinheads with the tin whistles.

"Wait here," said the men in unison. "We must announce you to Her Majesty."

"Oh, this is the palace and we are going to see the Queen!" whispered Ruth Ann anxiously.

Drawing aside the draperies that hid the end of the long hall from view, the two Pinheads put their whistles to their lips and blew once more the long shrill note. Then Deputy Stepit advanced into the inner chamber, announcing in a grand voice:

"Prisoners to see Your Majesty!"

"Show them in, please, Stepit," came the sweetest voice that Ruth Ann had ever heard.

The Pinheads drew the curtains wide to let the little girl and her friends into the throne room of Her Majesty, Queen of the Pinheads!

The audience chamber was lovely. Its walls were hung with fine silk scarves spun of every color of the rainbow. Although the room was spacious, there were no chairs or couches. None were needed—at least for the owner of the room.

For suspended from a wrought gold hook, in the center of the ceiling, hung the Ruler of all this Pinhead Country. She was nothing but a lantern—but oh, what a beautiful one!

Her body was a great round Japanese lamp with gorgeous chrysanthemums painted on it in white and gold. She had no feet, at least that Ruth Ann could discover, hanging below the beautiful round body. Above the round black rim at the top of the lamp rose a little face, the sweetest, most adorable face that ever an eye looked upon! The only face that Ruth Ann had ever seen that could in any way approach its loveliness was that of her own beloved Clara Belle, her favorite doll on Earth.

Her Majesty's face was pink and white like a lovely tea rose, with great blue eyes, a tiny, well-shaped nose and a mouth as pink as the inside of a sea shell. Over her head fell the shower of her hair in innumerable soft, golden curls.

"Oh, Your Majesty," exclaimed Ruth Ann, "you're . . . you're perfectly lovely!"

"Quite the nicest thing we've seen," added Whistle Stick, surprising them all by making a low bow to the lovely diminutive sovereign. "How did you happen to get mixed up with this Pinhead crowd . . . ?"

Here Deputy Stepit stopped him by making a fierce gesture toward him with his rubber hammer.

The Queen herself bowed and smiled at their compliments.

"So kind of you to like me," she returned, graciously. "You seem to be quite likable yourselves."

At this mark of favor from Her Majesty, Whistle Stick could not resist a look of triumph at the Deputy, who started forward at once to protest to the beautiful Queen.

"But Your Majesty, these three beings are prisoners. Have you forgotten the terrible plague that has befallen our country, that you speak so softly to them? Your Highness must beware of all strange beings!"

"Be silent, Stepit!" ordered the little Queen, with the first touch of haughtiness in her voice. "Am I not Ruler of the Pinheads, and shall I not manage my country in my own way?"

Stepit muttered something under his breath at this, but what he said was in such a low tone that no one heard it.

Again Whistle Stick could not restrain himself.

"I guess you'll behave yourself now for a while," he remarked in a whisper for the Deputy's benefit. "She knows how to show a fellow like you where he belongs!"

At this Deputy Stepit retained a sullen silence, but the look he gave Whistle Stick boded ill for the wooden man if ever the Deputy got hold of him.

Either the Queen did not hear the whispered quarrel of the two, or she was such a lady that she preferred to ignore it. At any rate she addressed her next question to Ruth Ann:

"Tell me. Who are you and what are you doing in my country?"

"Your Highness, we were blown up here, Whistle Stick and I, on the breath of the Green Blowster, mostly because we wanted to find Dukey Daddles. Lonesome was already here, kicked up by a mule. Dukey Daddles was my dog down on Earth, and he was run into High Country by a truck," continued the little girl.

"Oh," said Her Majesty. "I'm sorry, but I cannot help you in your search because I do not even know what a 'dog' is."

"Why that's all right," replied Ruth Ann. "You've been very kind to us anyway and we'll just keep on going, if you don't mind."

"Certainly, you may go," consented Her Highness.

"But Your Majesty," and again Stepit bounced forward to object. "It's dangerous to allow . . . "

"Stepit," commanded the Queen of the Pinheads, "you forget yourself! You may take your men and go!"

The Deputy was obliged to withdraw with his company, much to the delight of Whistle Stick who made a face at him and his men as they filed by.

The Queen, meanwhile, continued to address those whom she had just freed from captivity.

"Before you depart, wouldn't you like to rest for a short time? You must be tired from all your traveling."

"Oh," sighed Ruth Ann, "how kind of Your Majesty! That would be very nice! And while we rest, will Your Majesty be good enough to tell us how it was that you were made Queen of such warlike Pinhead People?"

"Why, yes, I can tell you that in a few words. My people chose me Queen because they love happiness above all, and I could make them happy by singing the 'Song of Joy.' Would you like to hear me?"

"We certainly would!" agreed Ruth Ann, Whistle Stick, and Lonesome, all in one breath. They were thoroughly under the spell of the lovely Queen's sweetness.

"Make yourselves comfortable on the floor then, and I'll call my breezes. I can never sing my best unless I'm swinging," she explained, "and it is my little breezes that swing me."

So saying, the gentle creature started to hum very low and sweetly. Immediately, lovely rainbow scarves began to sway to and fro, to and fro, as her soft breezes gathered from the four quarters to swing Her Majesty, Singing Lantern.

In a moment's time, her three spectators who were watching in amazement saw the lovely Queen herself begin to swing slowly back and forth. As she swung, she sang in a voice crystal clear and sweet:

"Breezes blow,

Soft and low,

Set the Lantern swinging,

Swinging.

In the room of Rainbow Scarves,

Set her swinging, singing,

Singing!

Tra-la-la-la-la-la-la,

Joy's the only song to sing!

Joy is such a lovely thing,

Scent like violets in the spring,

Tint like wild birds on the wing,

Sound like babies whispering,

Joy is such a lovely thing,

Joy's the only song to sing!

Tra-la-la-la-la-la-la,

There's no fear

To bring a tear,

There's ... no ... fear ... "

The audience of three friends, who had been enjoying the beautiful "Song of Joy" to the fullest, became suddenly concerned, for something had happened!

The sweet voice of the Queen began repeating:

"There's . . . no . . . fear . . .

There's . . . no . . . fear . . . "

over and over like a broken phonograph record.

"Oh, Your Majesty," cried Ruth Ann in instant sympathy, "whatever is the matter?"

"It's nothing, my dear. I'll be quite all right in a moment," answered lovely Singing Lantern. "I'll just have to start over again if you'll allow me. I'm sure that then I can finish the song as usual."

Once more the charming soft voice started:

"Breezes blow,

Soft and low . . . "

but when the Queen reached the words,

"There's no fear

To bring a tear . . . "

the clear voice came to a trembling stop and could not go on.

What was worse even than the sudden stopping of the song was the awful look of fear that came into beautiful Singing Lantern's eyes. She looked past Ruth Ann to the draperies at the entrance of the audience chamber!

"Quick," she whispered breathlessly to the little girl. "Look and see if someone is eavesdropping from behind those curtains! I saw them move just then, and if Deputy Stepit or any of his soldiers learn that I can no longer properly sing the 'Song of Joy,' we are all lost! They will depose me as their Queen and destroy you along with me!"

Immediately Ruth Ann looked as the Queen had directed, but the outer hall was empty. She could find not a sign of an eavesdropper.

Once more, the lovely color came back to Singing Lantern's face. As her calmness returned and she thanked Ruth Ann for her recent service, the friends were both surprised and shocked to see two great tears gather slowly in the Queen's beautiful blue eyes and glide down her soft cheeks!

"Oh, dear Queen," begged Ruth Ann, "please tell us what your trouble is. Perhaps we can help you!"

"It is beneath the dignity of the Queen to ask for help from anyone," she answered with a sob, "but I'm so alone and I am at my wit's end. I know not which way to turn! It's all the fault of the Terrible Fuzzy-Skinned Grumpus!"

"The Fuzzy-Skinned Grumpus!" exclaimed a puzzled Ruth Ann. "And what is the Fuzzy-Skinned Grumpus?"

"It's the plague that Deputy Stepit mentioned. It's a monster! It's a demon! It's an unutterably horrible creature that has come upon my people to devour and destroy them! I fear that I cannot sing of joy as long as there is such peril in the land."

"Let's destroy *it*, instead," stated Whistle Stick simply, since that seemed to him to be the easiest solution to the difficulty.

"Of course," joined in Lonesome Snake. "For once, Whistle Stick and I agree. We'll take care of it, immediately."

"Indeed, Your Majesty," said Ruth Ann. "You must let us help you. You have been so good to us that we are only too willing to rid your country of the plague!"

"But my dear friends," protested the Queen, "you have no idea of the strength and evilness of this creature, or you would make no such rash promises! Let me tell you how he came upon us, and then you can decide more thoughtfully as to whether or not you wish to accept the task of ridding Pinhead Country of such a monster!"

Chapter 16

Singing Lantern's Sad Story

 "ne day, the Pinheads were celebrating a festival on The Commons a short distance from the village," began Queen Singing Lantern. "My subjects were dancing and singing. Everyone agreed that we had never been in better spirits nor more enjoyed a celebration. There had even been some talk earlier in the day of doing away with Black Weeper and its services forever. There had been nothing to weep about for so long in our country that some of the officials felt it was a waste of goldfish eggs to keep the Black Weeper any longer in our employ.

"The Commons were strung for the occasion with long streamers of brilliant green leaves. There were singing lanterns hung upon these festoons, but of course no lantern so large or so beautifully colored as I," added Her Majesty with a tinge of pardonable pride.

"As usual, I was hung on a standard in the center of The

Commons, a gold standard, also decorated with millions of the bright green leaves. The scene was one of happiness and spring. The dancing was about over, and my people were crowding about my standard for the last happening of any of our festivals, the singing of the 'Song of Joy.'

"We had left a brave young Pinhead named Doodlebinker in charge of the village with instructions to report the least disturbance. We expected no evil tidings from him of course, as nothing had ever happened before.

"Just as I started to sing the 'Song of Joy,' however, much to our consternation and terror, we heard a great roar coming from our beloved village. As we looked in dismay toward our homes, we saw a mighty whirlwind strike them! One after another our houses tottered, and many of them fell with a great crash, utterly demolished. Some of us thought we could see a dark thunder cloud moving back and forth down the streets of the town. We were all appalled and paralyzed with fear. We did not know what to think—or what to do!

"Terrified whisperings began among the crowd. 'What could it be? Where was brave Doodlebinker? Perhaps he too had been destroyed!'

"I tried to keep on singing to quiet my people, but the murmurings grew louder and I could not sing above their continuous clamoring.

"At last, we beheld a welcome sight! It seemed Doodlebinker had escaped from the terror that had descended upon the village, for we suddenly made out his form running toward us at great speed. He came up to us finally, out of breath and with a great tear through one of his arms. He was hammerless and deadly white with fear.

"'To arms!' he cried. 'A monster has attacked us! A strange demon!'

"My people gathered around him with loud cries of sympathy and eager, horrified questions.

"'The plague demolished our homes with one blow of its heavy club,' the brave Pinhead responded in answer to their queries. 'The creature wears a great coat spun of fur and has four hands instead of two, each bearing four curved and sharp scimitars. It was with one of the scimitars that it tore this wound in my arm. Oh, Your Majesty,' he beseeched falling on the ground before me, 'what shall we do to rid us of this monster?'

"According to Doodlebinker's story, he had followed the monster as it left town and watched the creature take up its abode in one of the caves on the shore of Mirror Lake. Even at the distance that he was obliged to stand from the demon, he could see its great eyes shining like two red fires in the black depths of the den.

"'Who dares to go back with me and seize the plague in its lair?' challenged Doodlebinker, who was certainly the bravest of the Pinheads.

"At first not one of my people dared to take on so dangerous a task. But finally two other brave men, Dimpip and Doonquitz, agreed to go with Doodlebinker to the place where the monster was stationed.

"The rest of my people were afraid to go back to their homes, and as their houses had, most of them, fallen to the ground anyway, we all waited on The Commons for the return of our three heroes.

"After a period of waiting that seemed ages to us, we saw the three returning, but not with the same brisk walk that had carried them away from us. They were all walking slowly and sadly with their faces toward the ground, and Dimpip was limping painfully.

"When they arrived on The Commons, their faces wore expressions hitherto unknown among the Pinheads. Stamped on their features was great despair. They told their story in

whispers, as if even yet they could not believe its horror.

"'We tracked the monster to its cave at Mirror Lake,' said brave Doodlebinker, 'and he is even more terrible than I described to you. His eyes are sharp as the lightning!'

"'He should be called the Grumpus for he constantly growls low in his throat like distant thunderings,' said Doonquitz, in an awed tone.

"'And his mouth is full of round white daggers,' added Dimpip with a groan. 'He caught my foot and tore a hole in it with one of them.'

"'But the worst report of all, Your Highness,' said Doodle-binker, 'is yet to come! For the monster says that if we do not have the fattest Pinhead baby in the country delivered to his door every morning for his breakfast, he will ruin our beautiful land completely and devour us all!'

"As Doodlebinker gave out these terrible tidings, sadness descended over the whole population, and sighs and cries came forth from the people. They dispatched Deputy Stepit with a large advance payment to Black Weeper, but even with his help, they could not keep their own tears from flowing. Where that very morning had been dance and song, there was now only sorrow and wailing. It was a pitiful spectacle.

"Slowly we all trooped back to our village in solemn procession and assembled in the throne room of my palace, which had miraculously escaped destruction. There we discussed what was best to be done.

"Finally, it was decided to sacrifice the chubbiest Pinhead baby for the good of the land and the rest of the people. Families who had bragged that they had the fattest, healthiest babies in the country denied their former statements vigorously. They did not want to feed their beloved little ones to the Terrible Grumpus for his breakfast, and who could blame them?

"At last Doodlebinker spoke again. 'Your Majesty, since no one is willing to sacrifice his child for the sake of the country, let us wait one day and see what the monster does in return for our disobedience. His punishment may not be as horrible as he promised.'

"This suggestion won the favor of the people and it was with a hint of their former happiness that they returned to their homes and began to repair them after the havoc wrought by the Terrible Grumpus.

"The next morning there was no fat little Pinhead baby left before the lair of the monster, and nothing happened all that day. The people were greatly joyful and decided that the danger had been partly imaginary.

"That night however, as we lay sleeping, a great noise like growling thunder was heard on The Commons. My people awakened from sound slumber and watched with horror from their doors as an enormous dark shape descended upon the village. This time it attacked only one home, where lived Wee Dimpy and Tousle Top, two of the rosiest, happiest twins in all of Pinhead Country. With one blow of its great club, the creature dashed the house to the ground, and while their father and mother lay struggling in the ruins, the Grumpus carried off the twins in his teeth, that shone like round white daggers.

"That night was the real beginning of the desolation of my country," went on the soulful Queen, "for the next morning my people had become a changed people. The Grumpus had torn up and eaten all our beautiful green lawn in The Commons and had scattered our green festoons to the four winds. Since that time no more song or dance has been heard or seen in our village. Every morning a band of the bravest of the Pinheads carries one of our chubby little babies to the lair of the monster, who takes it into the black recesses of his den. It never comes out again, and we live in constant fear of what the horrible Grumpus will do next!"

"Your Majesty, how awful!" cried Ruth Ann, whose tender heart was aching with pity for the beautiful Singing Lantern and her subjects.

Exclamations of sympathy also rose from the lips of Whistle Stick and Lonesome. However, none of them had time for further words. A strange and ominous sound had arisen in the street outside!

Ruth Ann stepped to the front draperies and drew them apart. What she discovered put fear even into her stout heart. Coming rapidly down the street to the castle entrance, with their hammers swinging angrily over their heads, was a huge mob of Pinheads led by Deputy Stepit.

"Oh, Your Highness," cried Ruth Ann, "what ever shall we do? Here comes Stepit at the head of an angry crowd of Pinheads, and I'm afraid that he means the worst sort of mischief!"

"So, Stepit was eavesdropping when I thought I saw the curtains move," said Her Majesty. "Then I am afraid, dear friends, that it is all over for us. He has undoubtedly told his friends that my voice has forsaken me and that I no longer have the right to rule over the Pinhead People, for no longer can I sing the 'Song of Joy.' There is nothing else for us to do but calmly await the end as befits those of royal ancestry."

"I don't believe in waiting calmly if there's a fighting chance," cried Ruth Ann staunchly. "My grandfather fought in the Revolutionary War for our country! I believe in fighting when it's right to fight!"

"So do I!" shouted Lonesome.

"Me too," agreed Whistle Stick brusquely.

"Oh my dear, dear friends," said the Queen in her sweetest voice, "how brave you are! But as you see, I cannot do battle. I am hooked to the ceiling and cannot help you in any way. It is not fair for me to accept your sacrifice."

"Don't worry, Your Majesty," begged Ruth Ann. "You were kind enough to free us when we were strangers captured in your land, and we are only too glad to try to protect Your Highness now that your people have turned against you."

"It is really quite a privilege," said the snake, courteously.

"Quite so," agreed Whistle Stick without his usual gruffness.

The citizens led by the villain Stepit were already clamoring at the palace door. Shouts came to the friends in the throne room.

"Down with Singing Lantern! Up with Deputy Stepit!"

In an angry wave, the Pinheads surged in through the door, and tearing aside the draperies, rushed into the presence of the lovely Queen. They paused for a moment in surprise, for Ruth Ann, Whistle Stick, and Lonesome Snake had formed a semi-circle about Singing Lantern and stood there ready to defend their beautiful friend, to the end if need be.

Lonesome held his head forward as if to strike. There was something very formidable, too, in the way that Whistle Stick had doubled up his stiff fists to meet the attack. Ruth Ann, who was looking indignantly at the unfaithful Deputy, was larger than any of the Pinheads and was a foe to reckon with on that account alone.

As the little men hesitated at the sight of the defenders of the Queen, shouts of derision came from Lonesome and Whistle Stick.

"What are you stopping for? Don't you like our looks?" demanded Whistle Stick, who was making ready to get in one good blow at Deputy Stepit before the hammer heads began to reach him.

"Come on in," mocked Lonesome. "We're the reception committee for Her Majesty!"

Doubts seemed to enter the minds of the Pinheads. They were not at all certain of what these strange beings might do. They might have magic powers of some sort. The Grumpus had already taken much of their courage from them. They began to whisper among themselves. At this show of weakness, Stepit became furious!

"Are you then a lot of cowards," he cried, "that you give up so easily? It will be a light task to dispose of these foolhardy creatures, and we shall tear Singing Lantern apart with our hammers. Then I shall govern you as a great people have a right to be governed!"

Even as the evil Deputy spoke, Whistle Stick found the chance for which he had been waiting. As Stepit stuck out his chest with his proud speech, the little wooden fellow hit him a blow on his jaw that knocked the Pinhead completely over. He rolled on his round body almost into the outer hall before he could pick himself up. He was in a towering rage.

"Before you show your Pinheads how they ought to be governed," said Whistle Stick, boldly, "I thought I'd show them how a villain like you ought to be treated."

At this, someone in the crowd of Pinheads giggled; the sound of which made Stepit even wilder with rage. He leaped in front of the mob and began to upbraid them angrily.

"What sort of a people are you? Are you willing to let a Queen rule over you who can no longer sing her 'Song of Joy?' Are hundreds of you willing to be made a joke of by three strange creatures who dare face us with no weapons? Shall we let our babies be eaten every day and do nothing?"

It was this last argument that decided the Pinheads. As Deputy Stepit ceased speaking, mutterings again arose to an angry roar in the Pinhead ranks.

"You're right, Stepit! We're getting nowhere with Singing Lantern as Queen! Let's charge the newcomers and tear the Queen to pieces with our hammers!"

Led by Stepit, the bloodthirsty troops closed in on Ruth Ann and her two courageous friends, striking blow after blow with their hard rubber weapons. The three fought valiantly, but numbers were against them, and at last they fell under the hail of hammer blows. In a short time, they found themselves trussed up securely in stout cord like partridges ready for the poultry market, tied hand and foot.

"You're not so smart, now, are you?" jeered the mean Deputy as he gave poor old Whistle Stick a hard stomp on his foot.

"What'll we do with them now, men?" he asked, addressing himself to the others.

Loud cries came from various parts of the mob:

"Throw them to the Grumpus!"

"To the monster with them!"

"Hear! Hear! That's wisdom! Let the Terrible Grumpus eat *them* instead of our chubby babies!"

"To the demon with them! Perhaps *then* he'll leave us in peace for a few days!"

"Have mercy," pleaded the sweet voice of Singing Lantern, whose tears were streaming down her face. "I do not ask pity for myself, but rather for these visitors in our land who are my friends and who mean us no harm."

Deputy Stepit laughed mockingly.

"They're not so harmless as you think," he scoffed. "You didn't feel the force of their fists as we did, and the strength of their arms. We'll get rid of them first, my lovely Queen, and then we'll take care of you!"

The cruelty in his voice made Ruth Ann shudder. Whistle Stick tried to wrest his arms loose from his bonds to get in another good blow at Stepit. Lonesome Snake wiggled, too, in a vain effort to free himself. The Pinheads had done their roping securely and the friends were powerless to render more assistance to the gentle sovereign.

Half pushing, half rolling the captives, the little men began their short journey to the lair of the Terrible Grumpus. The friends were forced through the hall, down the palace walk, and through a side street to the banks of Mirror Lake. The lake sat in a deep basin, with high sides that rose for some distance perpendicularly from a narrow strip of beach.

The captives were given no time for observation, however. Stepit and his followers were too anxious to wreak their ill feelings upon the lovely Singing Lantern. With scant ceremony, they gave the three friends a push and a shove and sent them unceremoniously down the sheer drop of several feet to the lake, near the lair of the Terrible Fuzzy-Skinned Grumpus!

Chapter 17

Terrible Fuzzy-Skinned Grumpus

fter their sheer drop over the side, the three friends rolled over the strip of sandy beach almost to the lake itself, before they came to a stop.

"Thank goodness for a small favor," grunted Lonesome, as at last they ceased their rolling within a stone's throw of the clear water. "The trip over these rough beach pebbles has done me a service!"

With a wiggle and a squirm he wrested free of his bonds and showed the others. The rough stones had worn through the stout cord, and it had torn apart quite easily with his effort, leaving him free. In a moment he was working at the ropes that still held his friends firmly tied. Soon all three were free, stretching and straining to bring back the circulations that the cruel Pinheads had almost cut off with their tight bonds. They took their first keen glance around to see just what could be done about their desperate plight. Their situation did seem hopeless!

"There isn't the least possible chance of escape!" declared Whistle Stick with an air of conviction.

"We are rather like mice in a trap about to be fed to a huge cat," agreed the snake.

"And yet the Pinheads must know some way back and forth from the lake to the upper shore," murmured Ruth Ann, half to herself.

"That's so!" assented Lonesome with a tinge of hope in his voice. "And so must the Terrible Grumpus. Remember he must have gotten up out of this basin the night he stole the Pinhead twins!"

"We'll have to look about and see what we can see," suggested Ruth Ann. "But let's rest just a moment first. I don't mind confessing that I'm a trifle tired after our battle with the Pinhead mob."

"What a crowd of idiots they were," grumbled Whistle Stick, "to truss us up like fowls and throw us into this hole!"

"They may not be so idiotic," returned Lonesome. "They know more about the Grumpus than we do, and I have an idea that he's far from an idiot. I'll wager that he'll give us plenty of excitement!"

"It's horrible to think that we're here in the power of that monster and can't get away," shuddered Ruth Ann, "but let's not worry about him quite yet. It's really quite lovely here for a time, and I do not believe we need fear the Grumpus until night comes, anyway."

Indeed, the little girl spoke truly when she said it was a lovely scene upon which their eyes rested. There was comfort in the sight of the body of clear, cool water. On three sides of the lake, smooth green felt lawn ran abruptly up the steep sides to the higher edge and numerous small green bushes grew near the water's brink. However, on the side farthest from Pinhead Village, no green showed at all. A rock formation rose sheer from the very water's edge. It was somewhere among these rocks that the lair of the Terrible Grumpus was concealed.

For a few moments, the friends sat in silence, taking in the surroundings. The little girl then rose and took a step toward the lake.

"It ought to be restful to wade for a while," she explained. "The water of the lake isn't at all like Incorrigible River. It's wonderfully clear and smooth, without even the tiniest ripple!"

She ran a step or two and tried to push one foot into the gleaming water. At her gasp of astonishment, Whistle Stick and Lonesome came running up to her.

"Look!" cried Ruth Ann. "It isn't water at all! It's glass!"

"Undoubtedly that's why it's called Mirror Lake," suggested the snake.

"More imitation!" added Stick.

Examining the lake more closely, the trio found that it was actually just a huge mirror that reflected perfectly their three faces as they bent over to inspect it.

"Well," sighed Whistle Stick, "what else could you expect of Pinheads!"

Here a sudden exclamation from the snake made the others look in his direction.

"Have you noticed these pebbles?" he was saying. "I've gathered some of them up in my hand, and without a doubt they are the petrified goldfish eggs with which Deputy Stepit pays Black Weeper. This is another sure sign that there must be some manner of escape from the bottom of this basin!"

"How I wish we could find out what it is!" sighed Ruth Ann. "We might then be in time to rescue lovely Singing Lantern. I'm dreadfully worried about her."

"So am I," concurred Lonesome.

"There's nothing agreeable about that Deputy," added Whistle Stick. "The Queen is probably in pieces already!"

"Oh," gasped the little girl. "I do hope not!"

"There's no telling!" groaned the stick. "These Pinheads are an impossible people."

No sooner had Whistle Stick finished speaking, than the friends forgot their anxiety over the lovely Queen, for they were facing a new problem of their own. Suddenly the glow that made the daylight of the country went out as if someone had turned it out with an electric switch. The trio was left in total darkness!

"Well!" muttered Whistle Stick, "if this is the way dark comes to Pinhead Land, it's just one more reason why I like Earth better."

"I never knew night to come so swiftly!" Ruth Ann whispered fearfully. "I suppose now we can expect the Terrible Grumpus at any time! I did think we'd have a little time to prepare for him. What shall we do? Do you suppose that we would stand a better chance of subduing him if we could surprise him with an attack before he knows that we are in Mirror Lake Basin?"

"That's quite possible," conceded Lonesome. "There is something about a surprise attack that takes one off guard and generally proves successful."

"Anything is better than sitting around waiting to be devoured—or worse," grumbled Whistle Stick.

So having decided to carry the war into the enemy's country, the three friends began to creep very stealthily about the lake shore, being careful to keep on the water's brink, in order to arrive by the shortest possible route at the den of the Fuzzy-Skinned Grumpus.

As their eyes became more accustomed to the deep darkness, they were able to make out the outline of the lake and then, looming ahead of them, the shadowy rock formation where their hidden enemy was lurking.

Nearing the den, they proceeded more slowly and cautiously.

"What'll we do when we find the lair?" asked Ruth Ann, in a whisper to the others.

"Why not find big rocks and try stoning the creature with them when he comes forth?" suggested Lonesome.

"That does sound like a reasonable plan," said Ruth Ann, still whispering.

"It sounds so reasonable that I don't understand how *he* happened to have it," said Whistle Stick in a throaty mutter.

"Hush! Not so loud!" warned Ruth Ann, "We're almost there!"

In total silence, the little group crept along with the craggy rocks towering close beside them.

Suddenly . . .

"Look! Look!" exclaimed Ruth Ann in a tense whisper. "Isn't that a flicker of light coming through that wide fissure in the rocks?"

Stopping stock still in their stealthy journey, the three surveyed the rock wall with keen interest. Sure enough, coming from the opening between the rocks was a glimmer, as from candles far in its depths.

"Surely this must be the monster's den!" observed Ruth Ann with conviction. "Let's find the largest stones we can handle and take up positions at the crevice as Lonesome suggested. Perhaps we can surprise the Grumpus and secure him before he has a chance to strike back!"

Noiselessly, the three crept the few feet from the shore to the rock wall. As they approached, they succeeded in picking up several large stones that had evidently broken from the wall.

They decided on their respective positions. Whistle Stick took up his place at the right of the crevice, with Lonesome on the left. Ruth Ann began to climb as quietly as she could to a vantage point immediately over the fissure in the rocks. She, however, was hampered by carrying the biggest stone of the three.

"If I'm lucky enough to reach that flat landing above the crevice," she whispered back to her friends, "we can throw a rock down on the monster as he rushes out. That may stun him so he will be completely in our power."

No sooner did these hopeful words leave Ruth Ann's lips than she uttered a shrill little scream. The brittle rock ledge was giving way under her feet, and a shower of small rocks and pebbles was sliding down before the fissure like a miniature avalanche!

"Look out below!" warned Ruth Ann, thoughtful of her friends even in the extremity of her own peril. "I'm coming! The rocks are giving way under my feet and I can't hold on any longer!"

As Ruth Ann spoke, there was another slide of rocks and pebbles, and she shot out past the crevice to land upon the ground immediately in front of the lair with a dull thud.

Instantly, from within came a sound that drove the blood from the hearts of the three friends. Issuing from the fissure was a mumbling, grumbling growl, swiftly drawing nearer to them. The monster had heard the falling stones and Ruth Ann's scream as she fell!

"The Grumpus!" yelled Whistle Stick and Lonesome together. "Quick! Perhaps there is still time for the three of us to run and hide from him!"

Their hope was in vain. As they spoke, a black mass, like

a thunder cloud, flung itself through the crevice, straight upon the little girl who was struggling to rise from where she had landed, having been covered with rocks and stones!

"Stone him! Stone him!" shouted the snake excitedly. "Perhaps we may be able to save Ruth Ann!"

"You idiot!" shouted back Whistle Stick. "How can we stone him? We're bound to hit Ruth Ann as often as we hit the Grumpus, if we do!"

Suddenly, the mumbling, grumbling growls of rage ceased! Instead, there began to emerge from the terrible monster's throat short, sharp, staccato grunts of real pleasure! To the amazement of the spectators, the Terrible Grumpus and the little girl began to hug one another excitedly while the demon kept up his staccato grunts and Ruth Ann laughed and cried and cried and laughed, all at the same time!

"Oh, Whistle Stick! Oh, Lonesome! The Fuzzy-Skinned Grumpus isn't terrible—he isn't a monster at all—he's my own blessed Dukey Daddles!"

In a daze, Whistle Stick and Lonesome approached the two.

"It is indeed an Earth dog," stated Whistle Stick in complete amazement.

"So it is," agreed the snake. "Much as I've disliked the creatures in the past, I can say with all honesty that I am very glad to see this one!"

"Amen to that!" assented the wooden man.

As the two came up to her, Ruth Ann rose and greeted them joyfully. "Isn't it just too good to be true! Instead of being eaten alive by the Terrible Grumpus, we discover the monster is the very friend that we've been hunting through High Country to find! Dukey Daddles, meet my two very best friends, besides yourself, of course, Whistle Stick and Lonesome Snake!"

"Happy to meet you, I'm sure," barked Dukey in his abrupt way, giving each of them his paw to shake. "How did you happen to land up here?"

"Well," answered Whistle Stick, "it's a long story, but Ruth Ann and I were blown up here by Green Blowster."

"I was here already," explained the snake. "I had been

kicked up by a mule, and I tell you, I was mighty lonely until Ruth Ann and Whistle Stick came along."

"I can certainly sympathize with you in that feeling," barked Dukey Daddles. "I thought I'd die of loneliness until I hit on a plan of getting the Pinhead babies."

"Dukey Daddles," scolded Ruth Ann, "how could you eat those fat little Pinhead babies for breakfast? That's the only report that I've heard of you that disturbs me."

"Now, you didn't think I'd really eat them, did you?" said Dukey in a hurt tone. "I just said that I was going to eat them so that I'd have a thoroughly bad reputation. That way the Pinheads would be so afraid of me that they would not dare harm me. If you'll step inside my house—I've a surprise in store for you!"

With Dukey Daddles in the lead, the little group crept on hands and knees through the crevice and found themselves in a long subterranean hall. From one end came the flickering light that had first assured the friends that they had found the lair of the Grumpus.

Slowly traversing the hall, they found that it widened out at the inside end into a large and comfortable underground room. It was lighted by a strange phosphorescent glow from the rocks that lined the inside. Dukey had built a rough grate of big rocks, inside of which he had set a burner of petrified goldfish eggs that were smoldering very much like Earth coal.

Over the floor of the room was spread a carpet of green felt that Dukey had torn from the Pinhead Commons. And there on the soft carpet was a good round dozen of the most adorable Pinhead babies!

They were tumbling over one another in their play, laughing and gurgling with fun. Some of them were building with blocks that Dukey had brought them for playthings from the village houses that he had accidentally knocked over with his tail.

"Dukey, aren't they the cutest things that ever were!" cried Ruth Ann as she picked up two of the tots and began to cuddle them in her arms.

"Yes ma'am, they are!" barked Dukey with fatherly pride. "I never could have stood this country without them. You know how I love children, and I've always been used to being around them."

"Yes, I know," assented Ruth Ann. "You'll forgive me, won't you, Dukey Daddles, for ever doubting you? Why, this room is as cozy as can be."

"I always have a fire in the evenings," Dukey explained, "because I'm afraid that the babies will be cold without one. The nights here are rather chilly. Now, if you'll just excuse me for a moment, I'll put my family to bed and then we can talk without interruptions."

So saying, Dukey began to carry the babies very carefully,

one at a time, and place them in a long bed carpeted with innumerable bright calico leaves, making it a soft resting place. Before he put them down, he swung them gently between his teeth for a moment. The lulling motion caused the babies' merry little eyes to close, and in a twinkling, each lovely tiny Pinhead fell fast asleep.

"That's the duty I like most of any that I have during the day," sighed Dukey contentedly as he finished tucking in the very last baby. "I'm always sorry when it's finished.

"Now, I daresay you all want to know what's happened to me since I was run into this country by that truck. So if you'll just settle yourselves comfortably, I'll tell you."

Whereupon, Ruth Ann, Whistle Stick, and Lonesome Snake curled up on the rug in the soft warmth of the fire from the petrified goldfish eggs and prepared to listen to Dukey Daddles's story.

Chapter 18

Dukey Daddles's Story

"fter that terrible truck ran me into High Country," began Dukey Daddles, as he settled himself comfortably beside his friends, "I found myself at the gate to the Heaven of Lucky Dogs.

"Now, this heaven has a high wall around it so that I couldn't see what was on the other side. I ran along the wall until I came to a sort of high bench on a platform, and there sat St. Bernard, keeping watch over the entrance.

"'Hello, there!' said St. Bernard, looking down at me from his height. 'How did you get up here?'

"I told him about my accident with the truck, and he said that I had been very lucky to get such a swift ride into his kingdom.

"'Have you any vices?' he asked.

"Of course, I had to tell him that I was fond of chewing up shoes and the rockers on wicker chairs and had been punished often on Earth for such behavior. I had to confess, too, that I loved to run beside automobiles, barking at and worrying the drivers.

"'Well,' considered St. Bernard, 'those really are not very wicked sins. Are they all you can think of?'

"'So far as I know,' I replied, 'they are all that were ever brought to my attention in Earth life.'

"'How about your qualifications for the Heaven of Lucky Dogs?' asked St. Bernard. 'Have you more virtues than you have vices?'

"At that I was rather embarrassed, for no good dog wants to tell the nice things about himself. But St. Bernard insisted, and finally I did tell him that I loved children and home life and had always been very careful not to associate with undesirable playmates.

"St. Bernard seemed very pleased, especially with my not keeping company with naughty playmates.

"'You are a well-mannered dog,' he remarked, 'one of the kind that we are always glad to welcome among the Lucky Dogs. Now if you'll just give me your license number, you may enter at once!'

"At this request for my license number, cold chills began to creep up and down my spine.

"'But I'm not old enough to have a license,' I barked. 'Down on Earth, licenses are not required for dogs under six months old.'

"When I said that, St. Bernard looked at me very closely over his spectacles.

"'Are you going to try to make me believe that an Airedale your size is under six months old?' he asked with reproof in his growl.

"'But I'm not six months old,' I repeated. 'I'll not be six months old until the nineteenth of next month.'

"Still, disbelief showed itself on the kind face of St. Bernard. 'Have you a copy of your pedigree with you?' he asked. 'Or your birth certificate?'

"In vain I protested that I had been run into High Country too quickly to be bothered with copies of pedigrees or birth certificates.

"St. Bernard was unrelenting. 'Until you can establish

your age as that of a dog under six months old by some reliable proof or witness, you cannot enter into the Heaven of Lucky Dogs!'

"That was his final decree."

Here Dukey Daddles paused to wipe away a tear.

"So," he continued pathetically, "I had to become a wanderer upon the face of High Country. I didn't know where to go when the gate of my own 'people' was locked against me. I've traveled here and I've traveled there, trying to find someplace where I could be comfortable, but no place I've seen has suited me.

"Finally, as you know, I came to the Land of the Pinheads. I sauntered through their village one afternoon when they were holding a festival on The Commons. I accidentally knocked over a great many of their houses with my tail, but they thought it was a fierce club that I had used to assault their town. I was obliged to scratch their watchman, Doodlebinker, on the arm with my claw when he attacked me viciously with his hard hammer.

"You know what has happened since then as well as I do. I fought off three of the Pinhead champions who followed me down to Mirror Lake Basin. I then got the idea of having them deliver a baby to me each morning to overcome my loneliness and to frighten them into letting me be. At night I issued forth from my home and collected such things as the felt and calico leaves and the blocks to make my babies more comfortable.

"That's my story up to date," finished Dukey Daddles.

"But Dukey," cried Ruth Ann determinedly, "we're not going to have your story end as unhappily as that. Now that I'm here, I can go with you to the Heaven of Lucky Dogs and swear to St. Bernard that you're only five months old and don't need a license!"

Dukey threw himself upon her in joyful delight and licked her face three times to show his utter pleasure.

"How good of you," he barked. "I really hate to trouble you, but of course St. Bernard will believe you, and then he'll open the gate for me, and I can get in where I belong—with my own 'people.'"

"You'll come with us, won't you?" Ruth Ann asked Whistle Stick and Lonesome.

"Well, I've got no hankering to stay here with this Pinhead crowd, as you know," grumbled the stick. "As far as I am concerned, anywhere is better than here!"

"Of course I'll go," consented Lonesome Snake.

And so it was settled.

Dukey rose, and in two hops and a jump, crossed the room and ran swiftly up an almost perpendicular incline at the far end. Small gravel pebbles loosened and fell under his paws, but his sharp claws held in the ground, and he reached the top of the narrow passageway. There he removed something from the ceiling with his teeth, and instantly the room below, where his friends stood watching, was flooded with a pale light that dimmed the phosphorescence of the walls.

"You see," Dukey explained, "as I already surmised, it's getting daylight."

"Dukey, is that the way into the upper shore of Mirror Lake?" asked Ruth Ann. "We looked everywhere when we were thrown down here, but couldn't discover the hint of an exit."

Dukey leaped back beside her.

"Well, this is the way *I* come and go," he explained through his teeth, which were still carrying the portion he had removed from the roof.

This round piece, that had been in the opening in the ceiling, he handed to Ruth Ann and her companions, who examined it for a moment in silence.

"You see, it's a piece of glass out of Mirror Lake," Dukey Daddles continued. "I bit it out where it wouldn't show and stuck it up for a sort of window at the top of this steep tunnel. I dug the tunnel so that I could get into Pinhead Land whenever I wanted to. None of the Pinheads have discovered this secret passage of mine yet, so whenever I want anything in the village, I simply lift the glass out, and there I am right at The Commons!"

"Oh, Dukey Daddles, how perfectly splendid!" Ruth Ann

shouted with glee. "Here you have an exit all ready for us. Why we could start out right now!"

But at this suggestion, Dukey shook his head.

"If you please, I'd like to wait until the regular morning baby is delivered. It would be too bad to leave the little fellow all alone down here on the beach with no one to take care of him. If we wait for just awhile, we can take the new baby up to the upper shore with the others and leave them all on the palace doorsteps. I believe we could manage to lift them all out of the opening one by one, and then carry them to the village in the felt rug as if it were a hammock."

"I guess we could do that," replied Ruth Ann, "but tell us Dukey, how do the babies get here. Could we leave the basin of Mirror Lake the same way that the babies come down to its lower shores?"

"No, you couldn't," stated Dukey, positively, "and I'll show you why in just a while."

As the dog spoke, there came a squeak and a squawk from somewhere outside and Dukey started on a run through the underground hall to the outside.

"It seems earlier than usual, but I'm quite sure that the baby is on the way now!" he called back to them. "Follow me!"

Creeping swiftly on hands and knees, the three others followed Dukey. As they reached the outside, they watched his paw point to the crest of the basin side. The squeak and the squawk had come from a miniature derrick that was being lowered into Mirror Lake Basin from above!

"That small derrick," Dukey told them, "is what the Pinheads use to hoist up the petrified goldfish eggs with which they pay Black Weeper. Up to the time that I completed my steep runway into the upper country, that derrick was the only mode of entrance or exit from Mirror Lake Basin. The Pinheads operate it from the top and I can always tell when it's coming on account of the squeaks in the machinery. It certainly needs oiling!"

As Dukey finished his explanation, the derrick came to rest on the basin floor and then, with another squeak and squawk, parted into two halves, each a scoop shovel. As it parted, the derrick deposited a figure on the lakeshore. The two parts of the derrick then joined again and rose swiftly to the upper country.

One look at the form left behind by the derrick and a cry of surprise resounded from the lips of the watchers. Instead of the appealing baby Pinhead that they were expecting to see, it was Doodlebinker, the bravest of the Pinheads. He was so tattered and torn that he was barely recognizable.

"I thought something unusual was in the wind!" barked Dukey, who was the first to recover from his astonishment. "It did seem too early still for the delivery of my breakfast baby!"

Doodlebinker tried to rise but fell back again to the ground, thoroughly exhausted. The four friends ran to him and tried to raise him between them.

"How terrible! How terrible!" he kept repeating over and over to himself as if in a daze.

A cold chill swept over Ruth Ann. "What is so terrible, Doodlebinker? Tell us quickly what has happened!"

"Oh," groaned the Pinhead, "I come to you for help, hoping that you may have escaped the Terrible Grumpus and can return with me to help rescue lovely Singing Lantern. I am so weak and faint, and I could not hold the derrick here. It has risen again to the upper shores and with it, our last hope of leaving Mirror Lake Basin!"

"Do not worry over the loss of the shovel, Doodlebinker," consoled Ruth Ann eagerly. "We know another way of escape from these lakeshores. But tell us quickly! What of the Queen? What of Singing Lantern?"

Brave Doodlebinker groaned again in deep despair.

"Her Majesty may already be dead!" he answered. "For yesterday afternoon, after throwing you to the Grumpus, Stepit and his cowardly mob returned to the village, surrounded the Queen, captured those of us who refused to be traitors to Her Majesty, and threw us into jail. Early this morning I escaped by a miracle and resolved to seek you out in the hope that you might have conquered the Terrible Grumpus and be able to return to rescue the Queen."

"Well, we didn't overcome the Grumpus," said Ruth Ann, "but much to our more-than-welcome surprise, we found him to be an old friend of mine. He will help us save Singing Lantern and restore her to the throne. Won't you, Dukey Daddles?"

"Most certainly I will!" asserted the dog. "I'll be only too glad for a chance to subdue those terrible Pinheads and knock some sense into them!"

"Be quick then; be quick!" urged the little fellow who was almost fainting from fatigue and fright. "They are burning lovely Singing Lantern this morning on The Commons, and then they intend to make Stepit their King!"

"If that's true, there's no time to lose," said Ruth Ann. "Hurry! Let's carry Doodlebinker into the room and let him watch the babies until we can send for them. We certainly do not want them in the village if there is going to be a battle."

"That's a splendid idea," agreed Dukey, "for Doodlebinker is in too weak a condition to help us anyway, and he can be very useful here."

So half walking and half resting limply on the arms of
Ruth Ann and Whistle Stick, the brave Pinhead was carried
to the entrance of Dukey's underground home and from there
was pulled and shoved through the small dark hall into the
comfortable living room.

In spite of his weakened condition, Doodlebinker
exclaimed with delight at the sight of the Pinhead babies when
Dukey Daddles showed them to him by pulling down their felt
bedcovers. They were still sleeping peacefully.

"They'll sleep quite late this morning," said Dukey,
"because I let them stay up a bit too late last night enjoying
themselves! They've been such a comfort! I'll be sorry to
give them up." There was a trace of tears in Dukey Daddles's
voice.

Ruth Ann patted him sympathetically on the shoulder.

"You've been a good father to them, Dukey," she said.
"We know that, and we know that they'll miss you as much as
you'll miss them."

Her words seemed to hearten poor Dukey tremendously,
and he barked his thanks.

"Come! Come! We must not forget Singing Lantern!"
broke in Lonesome.

"No! Let's give the Pinheads something to remember us by
that is *not* a pretty present!" growled Whistle Stick.

"That's right," agreed Ruth Ann. "We'd better start right now. Here Dukey, you go first; then I can push Whistle Stick and Lonesome up to where you can catch hold of them and pull them up through the opening and onto The Commons."

"Can you get up all right yourself?" asked Dukey with a bit of anxiety in his bark.

"Don't worry at all about me. I'm quite sure that I can make it."

Thus Dukey clambered hurriedly up the almost sheer side and soon disappeared through the ceiling onto the upper ground. The distance to the opening was greater than Ruth Ann had suspected. She found it necessary to lift Whistle Stick onto her shoulders and then hoist Lonesome up to where Whistle Stick could lift him, in turn, onto his shoulders. Dukey Daddles could then reach down from above and pull the snake through the opening to land safely beside him!

"Here's a fine business!" grumbled Whistle Stick, as the snake was finally carried to the surface. "How'll the two of us get up now? We never figured on the distance to the opening being so great. We're not close enough for Dukey to reach us now that Lonesome is gone!"

Dukey Daddles and Lonesome had already put their heads together on the problem. Scarcely a moment later, there appeared from the hole above something that looked like a great long cane, but what the two below discovered was really the snake. He had stiffened himself out in that shape so that his friends could take hold of his hook end and be drawn up easily into Pinhead Land!

Whistle Stick caught hold at once and was lifted out. Dukey Daddles then held Whistle Stick by the legs, who then held the snake down to Ruth Ann. She caught hold of her friend's curved head, and at last all four were reunited at the top.

They had all been so interested in the problem of their own escape from Mirror Lake Basin that they had forgotten, for the moment, Singing Lantern and her plight. However, the instant they faced about and took their first look toward The Commons, their blood ran cold!

Chapter 19

The Rescue of Singing Lantern

 he sight that met the eyes of the four friends was well calculated to strike terror in their hearts! On The Commons, near the spot where our watchers stood hidden from the Pinheads by a screen of bushes, the little folks were preparing the funeral pyre for their lovely deposed Queen.

Every Pinhead in the village seemed to be there, busily bringing branches from bushes and setting them on a great pile. Singing Lantern, hanging from her golden standard, looked on helplessly at these preparations for her execution. Even as Ruth Ann watched, two of the Pinhead guards, at an order from wicked Stepit, ran to the Queen, lifted her and her standard high in the air between them, and deposited her on top of the high brush pile!

Ruth Ann shuddered as she thought of the awful fate of their beautiful friend if they were unable to rescue her. They must act and act at once!

A plan for the rescue was at work in her mind. She turned and broke off a stick from one of the bushes near to her and borrowed Lonesome's prized bandana. She tied the bandana to the end of the stick like a signal flag. She then gave a few orders.

"Dukey Daddles," she directed, "suppose you proceed at once to the village. Watch there for signaling from my red flag. If I raise and wave it once, that means to demolish one street of Pinhead houses. If I raise it twice, it means to come back to The Commons. But if I hold my flag high and wave it frantically many times, it means that you must destroy the Pinhead village utterly and completely. You must then return at once to The Commons. Such a distress signal as that will mean there

is no longer any hope whatsoever of making peace with the villagers, and we shall have to do battle for the lovely Queen who has been so good to us!"

"Right-o!" barked Dukey, and without another word he set off at full speed for the village.

Ruth Ann turned to Lonesome Snake. "If you agree to my plan, follow Dukey to the village and free Dimpip and Doon-quitz. Recruit them to assure safe passage to and from Dukey's underground room, where you must swiftly go and bring out Doodlebinker and the Pinhead babies. Take the little ones to the throne room of the palace, and carefully conceal them until they are needed.

"Now," continued Ruth Ann to Whistle Stick, "you and I must hasten to The Commons and see if we can keep the Queen from this terrible fate that is about to overtake her!"

So saying, she and her friend made off toward The Commons on a run.

They arrived at the great funeral pyre in the very nick of time! The people were already grouping about their former Queen while Stepit, with an evil grin on his face, held aloft a burning torch, ready to set fire to the pile of brush.

"Farewell, my people," Singing Lantern was saying in her sad, sweet voice. "I am sorry that you no longer love me or want me for your Queen, but I forgive you with all my heart for the wrong that you have done me."

It was at this moment that Ruth Ann and Whistle Stick broke through the throng surrounding the pyre. Whistle Stick thrust up the flaming torch in the hand of Stepit, just as he stooped to set Her Majesty on fire.

"Stop!" cried Ruth Ann, flinging herself in front of the Queen. "Have you no sense, no justice? Why do you burn your good and beautiful Singing Lantern for the sake of a villain like Stepit? He means you harm instead of good! If he is your King, you will never be happy again!"

Stepit was wild with fury. He struggled to tear his arm away from Whistle Stick, but that gentleman was taking the greatest glee in holding the hateful Deputy as firmly as he could. It was impossible for the Pinhead to break away!

The people themselves looked at Ruth Ann in complete amazement. The last time they had seen her, she and her friends had been bound and thrown into Mirror Lake Basin to make a meal for the Terrible Grumpus!

They cowered away from her now, awed and astonished to see her alive and free.

"A magician!" they cried in fright. "A magician who has outwitted even the monster Grumpus!"

Ruth Ann had never expected this sort of reception. She decided to use the Pinheads' fear of her to the advantage of the dear Queen, who had shed a tear of joy at the sight of her friends. Ruth Ann stepped forward.

"You are quite right," she assented. "I am a magician; so is Whistle Stick; so is Lonesome Snake; and so is our friend, the Terrible Fuzzy-Skinned Grumpus!"

At her mention of the last name, the Pinheads retreated a few steps with exclamations of horror breaking from their lips.

"Even now," Ruth Ann continued, ". . . even now, the Grumpus is awaiting orders from us as to whether or not to destroy your village. Behold my scepter of power!"

As she spoke, she held forward the stick to which she had tied the red bandana.

"She is speaking untruths," broke in Stepit. "She may have escaped unharmed from Mirror Lake Basin, but the Grumpus is not her friend. She is lying to you! She has no magic powers, nor have her companions. She is trying to trick you to save her friend, the Queen!"

With the words of evil Stepit, Ruth Ann saw that the people were again divided. Some were afraid of her and thought that she was telling the truth, while others were allying themselves with the Deputy against her and the Queen. The little girl took the only way out.

"Very well, then," she cried out loudly, "I do not like to do what I must because it will cause you pain, but those of you who do not believe me must be taught. Therefore— watch me!"

Speaking thus, she held the bandana high above her head and waved it once, looking at the village as she cried aloud:

"Rub-aduba, rub-aduba,

Mighty Grumpus, with your cluba,

Strike the little Pinhead towna,

Smite it downa—smite it downa!"

At the terrible words of her incantation, the Pinheads crowded together, frightened and confident now that Ruth Ann was the magician that she had claimed to be. As they glanced timidly at their little town, they saw their worst fears confirmed. Dukey Daddles, true to the order that Ruth Ann had given him, had been watching eagerly from the village, and the moment that he saw the red flag waved once, he demolished a whole street of Pinhead houses!

Immediately, the sight threw the Pinhead population into a panic. They threw themselves to the ground before Ruth Ann in abject fear. Even Stepit could not disbelieve the sight from his own eyes nor the sounds of destruction that came from the town. He was in such terror that his legs bent under him, and he fell before Whistle Stick, grasping the wooden man's legs and begging to be saved!

Of course, Ruth Ann and Whistle Stick were overjoyed at the turn events had taken. They could have danced and sung with glee. They knew, however, that they must act with dignity before the people or they would lose standing, so Ruth Ann said in a very grand manner:

"Now that you have admitted the truth of my words, will you again accept lovely Singing Lantern as your Queen?"

"Anything you command! Anything!" agreed the people eagerly. "Only summon back the Terrible Fuzzy-Skinned Grumpus and protect our village and ourselves from total destruction!" In their words of appeal, Stepit's voice was raised higher than any other!

Ruth Ann lifted the flag and waved it twice over her head, thus signaling Dukey back to The Commons. "I am certainly glad that you will listen to reason," she continued sternly, again addressing the Pinheads. "Untie Her Majesty!"

Instantly, a great mob of the little people stepped forward eagerly to do her bidding. In a second the lovely Singing

Lantern was free, and with a sigh of happiness, thanked her subjects for unbinding her and Ruth Ann and Whistle Stick for their brave rescue.

"Now you, Stepit and Whistle Stick, proceed ahead of us to the throne room of the palace," said Ruth Ann. "All the Pinheads follow in an orderly procession, four abreast. There is a surprise awaiting you at the castle.

Dukey's arrival at this point threw the people into temporary commotion, but the confusion was soon quelled and the line formed. With Her Majesty between them, Stepit and Whistle Stick headed the crowd as they marched to the palace with lusty shouts of:

"Long live our Queen!"

"Long live the magicians!"

When they reached the castle, Ruth Ann and Dukey slipped in ahead of the others to where Lonesome had arrived with the three brave Pinhead soldiers and the little Pinhead babies. She was delighted to find all of them already in the throne room.

She waited there long enough to cover up the babies with their green felt blanket, for she wished to surprise the people with them. She then directed the waiting others to enter. Stepit and Whistle Stick burst into the room with Singing Lantern, followed by the rest of the Pinheads.

At first the people were afraid to mingle at all with the magicians, as they called them, particularly with the Terrible

Grumpus. But by the time that Stick and Stepit had re-hung the happy Queen and had seen that their three brave leaders, Dimpip, Doonquitz, and Doodlebinker, were talking merrily with the terrible monster, a great part of their timidity left them and they were even able to shout:

"Long live the Terrible Fuzzy-Skinned Grumpus!"

"And now," announced Ruth Ann, "in order that you may know that evil has finally left Pinhead Land, your lovely Queen will sing for you once more her 'Song of Joy.'"

At these words a burst of applause rose from the Pinheads, followed then by complete silence as Singing Lantern began to summon once again her breezes from the four quarters. Sweetly she sang, this time without a tremor or catch in her clear voice:

"Breezes blow

Soft and low

Set the Lantern swinging,

Swinging.

In the room of rainbow scarves,

Set her swinging, singing,

Singing!

Ruth Ann and the Green Blowster

Tra-la-la-la-la-la-la,

Joy's the only song to sing!

Joy is such a lovely thing,

Scent like violets in the spring,

Tint like wild birds on the wing,

Sound like babies whispering.

Joy is such a lovely thing.

Joy's the only song to sing!

Tra-la-la-la-la-la-la,

There's no fear

To bring a tear,

To the Lantern swinging,

Swinging.

In her room of rainbow scarves,

Joy itself is singing,

Singing!"

As the lovely voice ceased, shouts of happiness burst from Pinhead throats. Then, at a motion from Ruth Ann, Dukey, Lonesome, and the three brave guardsmen opened up the felt carpet and the little Pinhead babies rolled out, fat, rosy, and gurgling with laughter!

What a scene there was! Nothing like it had ever been seen before in Pinhead Land. Mothers and fathers grabbed their restored little ones with shouts of glee and everyone tumbled over everyone else in an ecstasy of happiness. The people shook hands with Ruth Ann, with Lonesome, with Whistle Stick, with the three loyal Pinhead guardsmen, and even with the Terrible Grumpus. The air resounded with cries of blessings on the lovely Queen and her faithful friends!

At last the people decided that they ought to leave and let Singing Lantern rest after her trying ordeal of earlier. They filed out with their babies, still shouting back praises of their ruler and vows of unending faithfulness to her.

Only Deputy Stepit lingered. There was fear on his face alone of all the Pinhead crowd. For his disloyalty to the Queen had started all the trouble. However, as he stayed behind in the throne room, uncertain of his fate, a sweet smile broke over the lips of Her Majesty, Singing Lantern.

"Do not fear, Stepit," she said in her clear and royal voice. "We all make mistakes and I forgive you willingly and completely. From now on you shall be one of my personal bodyguards!"

"Can't I give him just one swift kick, Your Majesty?" asked Whistle Stick, pleadingly.

At this request, the Queen of the Pinheads laughed merrily, but shook her head.

A great happiness shone on Stepit's face, and he knelt very low before Singing Lantern.

"Such action as yours befits a real Queen," he declared, "and I promise to serve Your Majesty faithfully and well, always!"

"He's not such a bad one at that," commented Whistle Stick gruffly. "I'd like to give him one good kick, but I must say that he knows when he's beaten."

"And now," said Ruth Ann, "seeing that Your Majesty is again in power, with the revolution all settled, we must be on our way!"

"Must you leave us?" cried the Singing Lantern with real regret in her voice.

"Indeed, I'm afraid that we must," answered Ruth Ann, "for we are going to take Dukey Daddles back to the Heaven of Lucky Dogs and swear to his age before St. Bernard. Already the scale that the Green Blowster gave me is turning darker and we *must* be back at the entrance to High Country before it turns black or we shall *never* get back again to Earth!"

Chapter 20

Concerning the
Official Transport

he Queen tried to conceal her disappointment by bravely smiling at the little girl.

"My only wish," said Her Majesty, "if you really must go, is that I could show my gratitude for the wonderful help that you have been to me!"

"Please don't mention it," replied Ruth Ann politely. "I can assure you that it has been only pleasure to serve one so sweet and lovely as yourself."

"Those are our sentiments too," spoke up Whistle Stick, Lonesome, and Dukey Daddles, all together.

"There is however, something that worries me a bit," confided Ruth Ann gravely. "As I said, the Blowster's scale is getting dark and we have no idea how long it will take us to get to the Heaven of Lucky Dogs. We simply must be back at the entrance to High Country before the Green Blowster needs his last breath and sinks back to the bottom of the pool!"

At the little girl's words, a light shone in the face of Singing Lantern.

"I have it!" she exclaimed. "I shall be able to help you some after all! The Official Transport of High Country lives not far from here. His wing caught in one of the castle turrets not long ago and I was able to send some of my people to release him. I know he'll be glad to help you!"

"That is splendid!" exclaimed Ruth Ann with delight. "How do we find his place?"

"The garage is on the outskirts of Pinhead Land not far from The Commons," directed the sweet Queen. "Just mention my name and that you are my friends."

"Thank you so much for your kindness, Your Majesty," said Ruth Ann. "And now I do believe that we had better be starting for we have a long, hard trip ahead and our time here is growing short."

"Goodbye to you all, my friends," called the Queen, "and good luck! If you ever have another chance to visit High Country, don't forget to make my palace your headquarters."

"Thank you, again. You can be sure that we would gladly accept your invitation," shouted the four friends as they waved joyously in farewell to Singing Lantern. Then they set out through the hall and into the streets.

How different was their passage through the Pinhead village this time from that first trip when they had marched along, guarded by Stepit and his men! Now they walked by houses, and the Pinheads rushed to their doorways to cheer them on their way! Some of the little mothers held out babies for them to kiss, the very babies that Dukey Daddles had cared for so carefully in his underground nursery. This last goodbye to his little charges was very trying to the puppy, and he hastily borrowed the red bandana to brush the tears from his eyes several times as the friends hurried down the streets.

Everywhere, they were greeted with shouts of praise. Showers of calico leaves were thrown before them, and a great mob of Pinheads followed them to say a last goodbye as they left the village.

Finally, they reached The Commons. There Ruth Ann and the others paused to set fire to the pyre that was to have been the burning place of the lovely Singing Lantern.

"It's just as well to have the thing burned down. That way it won't suggest any evil thoughts to the Pinheads," grumbled Whistle Stick. "No telling how long they'll keep their senses. Their heads are too small to hold anything long."

"My, what a terrible morning we had!" remarked Lonesome, wiping the perspiration from his forehead with his red bandana, as he lived the morning over in memory. "I've never been so frightened in my life, not even when we were running away from Incorrigible River!"

"I'll confess now that I was far from calm, myself," confided Dukey. "These Pinheads are peculiar people. You never know which way they are going to turn."

"I tell you, their heads are too small. That's what's the matter," Whistle Stick grumped, "and that evil little Stepit . . ."

"Now, now, I believe he means to be all right from this time on," interrupted Ruth Ann softly. "I don't see how anyone could be wicked with such a delightful Queen as Singing Lantern!"

They had reached the outskirts of The Commons, at last, and paused long enough to wave farewell to the Pinheads who had followed them to wish them good speed on their journey. As the little people dispersed to happy homes, the friends turned about to find the garage of the Official Transport.

It was not hard to find. As a matter of fact, the garage was in plain view from The Commons, and the only reason that Ruth Ann and the others had not observed it before was because their minds had been so concerned with other things. It was painted a fiery red, and over it was a great white sign with "Official Transport" painted on it in big black letters.

As the friends approached the double doors of the building, a strange sound came to their ears. "Ah—ssst! Ah—ssst! Ah—ssst!"

"Let's creep up closer and look through the window!" suggested Ruth Ann, bravely.

Very cautiously, they made their way to the small window

in the side of the garage. One glance inside and they drew back in amazement.

"Why the Official Transport is a huge flying fish and he's snoring!" chuckled Ruth Ann to her friends.

With keen interest, the four took another peep through the window and, sure enough, Official Transport was a huge flying fish, clumsily sprawled on a red plush couch inside the building! He was snoring regularly and noisily. The sound of his snoring was the mysterious "Ah—ssst!" that the friends had heard.

"It does seem a pity to disturb him," whispered Ruth Ann, "but if we are to make up any time at all on our trip, we'll simply have to get started!"

They all walked around to the front doors where Ruth Ann

knocked timidly at first, and then more vigorously.

At first the snoring kept right on, but finally the sound of knocking must have penetrated, for a fussy, squeaky voice came from the interior.

"Well, well, well!" it said. "Why the knocking? What will you have? What's all the rumpus about?"

"We came from the Queen of the Pinheads," shouted out Ruth Ann. "We need your help!"

"Well, well, well!" repeated the voice from the inside, "Why didn't you say so! That's a different matter . . . a very different matter!"

Immediately a scuffling set up inside the room and an instant later, a huge fish appeared in the doorway, clad in a robe and bed slippers.

"What can I do for the friends of Her Majesty?" he asked. "Anything to oblige Queen Singing Lantern! She did me a good turn one day and I'll never forget her kindness—no, never!" And grabbing the red bandana he blew his nose violently!

Snake snatched away his prized handkerchief with a muttered exclamation about the forwardness of *some* people. Fortunately, the fish did not overhear the remark.

"We are trying to reach the Heaven of Lucky Dogs," began Ruth Ann, "and we have only a very short time until we have to be back to Green Blowster's breath. Can you take us where we wish to go?"

"Well, well, well!" answered the creature, looking puzzled as he scratched his head thoughtfully behind his right fin. "I thought that I knew everyplace in High Country, but that's one I must have overlooked. If you'll step inside, I'll look at my map."

Ruth Ann and her friends followed Flying Fish into the garage.

"Just have a seat on the couch," he directed, "and if there's a Heaven of Lucky Dogs anywhere around, I'll find it in a jiffy!"

He drew a large pair of spectacles from his pocket and, putting them on, looked intently at a great map hanging on the wall.

"Here's Shadow Forest," he said, "and Incorrigible River, and yes, here's Pinhead Land but . . . wait a minute . . . wait a minute!" His finger moved aimlessly about and then suddenly settled with a decided swoop.

"Here it is, children! Here it is—Heaven of Lucky Dogs, right to the left of Cat's Canyon. My, my, that's a long way to go from here, but I guess we can make it in time."

"Please, Mr. Official Transport, fly as fast as you can," pleaded Ruth Ann. "We must hurry!"

Flying Fish hastily changed his slippers and robe for a pair of high boots and a uniform with a great white button in the coat lapel bearing the insignia "Flying Fish, O.T." Next he took an extra large drink of fuel from the container in one corner of the room and began to quickly button on his passenger basket. His preparations were simple and he was ready at once for departure.

"Climb in, children," he instructed, "and we're off!"

Swooping low so as to clear the top of the double doors, Flying Fish flew down and out of the garage and into the open country. He flew as a bird flies, and his great wings waved slowly up and down, as his great body shoved its way through the air and gained speed at every motion of his wings.

To the friends in the passenger basket, the experience was a delightful one. The air about them was warm. Far below they could see the floor of High Country, while back of them in the distance, gradually growing smaller and smaller, were the little homes of the Pinheads!

On and on through the air they flew, the fish moving so rapidly that after a time they could no longer make out any outlines on the ground below.

Dusk approached, and still the Official Transport kept on, apparently not tired at all with his exertions.

"We must be almost there!" he shouted back at his passengers. "If I'm not greatly mistaken, the blur of lights ahead is the very place that we're looking for!"

"Dukey Daddles," cried Ruth Ann, "aren't you excited! Just think, we're going to see St. Bernard and tell him that what you said about your age and the license was true and then . . ."

"And then," went on Dukey with tears of joy in his eyes, "I'll be accepted in the Heaven of Lucky Dogs and I can be happy for always!"

Ruth Ann and Dukey hugged each other rapturously.

"I'm slowing down for the descent," shouted Flying Fish. "Hold tight, everybody."

They all held tight to the basket sides as the great fish's wings flapped more slowly and more slowly and finally stopped. He floated rather than flew, gently down to a landing on the ground.

"Here we are," he declared. "Everybody out for the Heaven of Lucky Dogs. If you're only going to be a short time, I'll wait here and take you back on the return trip."

"Oh, Flying Fish, that will be good of you," replied Ruth Ann gratefully. "We'll try to cut our visit as short as possible, so as not to keep you waiting long. Come everyone! We must hurry!"

Chapter 21

Heaven of Lucky Dogs

he four friends had taken hands and run swiftly to the wall surrounding the Heaven of Lucky Dogs. Ruth Ann, who was always curious, passed her hand lightly along its surface. Then she exclaimed with the joy of discovery:

"Why, Dukey Daddles, you didn't tell me that the wall was made of dog biscuits!"

"I didn't consider them worth mentioning," answered Dukey with a sniff of disdain. "No respectable dog would choose them for food if they weren't forced upon him on Earth. I was delighted when I found that up here they are put to their proper use—building material!"

"It's not a very high wall," Ruth Ann remarked. "It's a wonder that the dogs don't jump out." The wall did barely reach to the top of Ruth Ann's head when she stood as tall as she could.

"My opinion of Dog Heaven," explained Dukey, "is that the idea of escape never occurs to the inhabitants. Things are made so pleasant here for the Lucky Dogs that they don't want to get away."

Gradually, the friends worked their way around the side and approached the front entrance of the heaven. Numberless little lights that reminded Ruth Ann of those on Christmas trees were strung on cords back and forth in many beautiful strands across the entire sky, making the scene a brilliant and festive one. The illumination was almost as bright as day. As the wanderers rounded the corner near the platform whereon sat St. Bernard, the huge Guardian of the Gate saw them and made frantic motions in their direction.

"Hurry up! Hurry up!" he shouted, waving his paws. "I'm about to close my office for the night!"

Ruth Ann and the others again broke into a run and soon traversed the distance between the corner and the box-like compartment from which St. Bernard conducted his business. When they reached him, he leaned far down over the wall to peer more closely at the strange foursome.

His eyes finally rested upon Dukey with the light of recognition.

"So there's *one* of you that I know, anyway," he said, with his kindly smile. "You're back, eh?"

"Yes sir," barked Dukey, "and this time I've brought along a witness from Earth who will assure you that I'm not old enough yet to have a license." There was a pardonable pride in Dukey's voice.

"Well, my lad, if I've misjudged you, nobody's sorrier than I," replied St. Bernard in a cheerful tone. "Who are these strange characters you have brought with you?"

"This is Ruth Ann," said the dog. "She was my playmate on Earth before I was run up here by that truck. And this is our friend, Whistle Stick. He and Ruth Ann were blown up to High Country on the breath of the Green Blowster, mostly because they wanted to look for me. And this," pointing to the snake, "is another friend, Lonesome Snake, who was kicked up by a mule and was already here when they arrived."

"I'm very glad indeed, to make the acquaintance of each of you," St. Bernard informed them as he leaned over to shake hands with each in turn.

Addressing Ruth Ann, he asked, "Are you ready to take an oath that your playfellow wears no license because he is too young for one according to Earth standards? He's certainly a big dog for five months." Again a hint of doubt crept into St. Bernard's kind voice.

He seemed assured a moment later by her steady statements. Ruth Ann remembered when Dukey was brought to her by a friend. At that time, he could just manage to toddle along on his legs with his fat little belly touching the floor. She told St. Bernard that Dukey was only two weeks and three days old then and had to be fed out of a bottle with warm milk.

"Well," St. Bernard said, "I'm certainly glad to know that Dukey didn't lie to me. He seemed such a good dog in every other respect that I was sorry to turn him away. But now . . . good gracious, I've almost forgotten! This is the night of our Annual Dog Show. You must all come in and be my guests and the guests of Dukey Daddles on his first night here. You will honor us, won't you?"

"Delighted!" shouted Ruth Ann, Whistle Stick, and Lonesome, all together.

St. Bernard took his great key and unlocked the gate for his new friends. It was a narrow gate, and not a very high gate for dogs. After Dukey had proudly entered, Ruth Ann and Whistle Stick had to go through on their hands and knees. Lonesome, not really being equipped for crawling, just wiggled on through.

When they straightened up once inside, an astonishing sight met their eyes. Around the dog biscuit wall were rows of kennels that stretched as far as the eye could see. They were all brightly colored, and above each kennel door was a round label with a number on it.

Dogs were running everywhere, dogs of all kinds: some with great collars around their necks, some with clown's caps on, and some wearing little blankets. There were Labrador Retrievers, Terrier mixes, Beagles, Poodles, Bloodhounds, and Great Danes, all varieties of dogs, purebreds, and mutts. All of them were hurrying hither and thither in preparation for the Annual Dog Show. The entire scene was one of frolic and festivity.

St. Bernard called out to a Dachshund that was rushing past with some colored streamers.

"Here, Pfeffernusse, will you please take Dukey Daddles and his friends to Kennel No. 344? You're lucky, you know," added St. Bernard, turning to Dukey, "because we really have very few first class kennels left. The one to which I am sending you and your friends would not have been vacant tonight, but two days ago Mukluk, who was occupying it, moved into other quarters so that she could be near an Australian Shepherd she is interested in. I hope you'll find everything comfortable."

As the St. Bernard finished, he handed Pfeffernusse a kennel key, and the little dog with a word of welcome, told the newcomers to follow her.

Soon they arrived at Kennel No. 344. Pfeffer, as she preferred to be called, opened the door with her key, and Dukey and the others followed her inside.

"I, too, hope you find everything in good order," remarked the little dog, as she opened a window in the side wall. "A kennel always smells a bit musty after it's been unoccupied for a day or two. I'll send Cleo, a Soft Coated Wheaten Terrier, with some extra towels and another cake of flea soap. If you'll excuse me now, I must go. I'm terribly busy with the Show, but I'll see you all later."

And with a flip of one of her long silky ears, Pfeffer was gone.

Dukey stared after her with interest. "Isn't she a delightful little creature? I keep getting happier and happier!" And with a wagging tail he added, "I hope I shall see Pfeffer often!"

As the others took stock of the interior of the kennel, they were very pleased that Dukey Daddles had found such excellent living quarters. There was a clean little cot in one corner with a soft mattress, and a closet for collars and blankets under the window, and a short washstand holding a clean towel and washbowl full of clear water. Beside the bowl on a tin tray was a new cake of the very best smelling flea soap.

"Let's get all cleaned up for the Dog Show," said Ruth Ann. "We haven't washed since we came to this country!" Suiting the actions to her words, the little girl washed her face and hands until they shone. Whistle Stick and Lonesome followed her example and lastly, Dukey Daddles did, too.

"Oh, Dukey, isn't it splendid," exclaimed Ruth Ann. "You'll be so comfortable here and have such fun!"

Dukey Daddles smiled happily, his tail still wagging.

At that moment a knock came on the door. Dukey opened it, and there stood St. Bernard, with a wreath of flowers about his neck and a guitar under one arm.

"You are to sit with me in my box," said St. Bernard in his kindly way. "I have come to get you. The orchestra is already playing the overture."

With exclamations of thanks for his hospitality, the four visitors followed St. Bernard to a great amphitheatre, evidently made for the Dog Show, with rows and rows of seats. On the bottom row were boxes with six seats each, reserved for distinguished dogs and fenced in by four boards.

"Pfeffer has kindly consented to be my guest, also," said St. Bernard, as the doxie hurried up to them. "We must be seated quickly, so that we do not miss any of the numbers."

They all sat down, and Dukey, with joy apparent, held a chair for Pfeffer and then seated himself beside her.

The orchestra was soon finished with the overture, and the special feature numbers of the program began.

The friends were both surprised and delighted to find

that the first number on the bill was to be played by St. Bernard, who stepped in front of the spectators and began a guitar solo that he had composed himself, called "Every Dog Has His Day."

He was greeted with great applause by the Lucky Dogs. He was evidently a great favorite.

Next, a Collie-mix named Hazzard gave a wonderful performance with a company of trained fleas.

"I tell you," remarked St. Bernard, "it does my soul good to see any dog make fleas hop and jump about through rings. Do you remember how it was on Earth?" Both he and Dukey sighed at the memory.

Then two Mexican Hairless dogs danced the tarantella with so much vim that they had to give a tango as an encore.

Ruth Ann was delighted and applauded and applauded!

"Fine program!" stated Whistle Stick, shaken out of his customary grumpiness.

"They certainly have a lot of talent up here," agreed Lonesome.

They were interrupted by the blare of a great horn blown by a Belgian Sheepdog, who was apparently the leader of the orchestra.

"I have an announcement to make," he growled in his deep voice. "Before we have the Grand March that is the number scheduled next, we must choose the King for the rest of the evening, one who will also lead our Grand March. Nominations are now open. Those nominated will please take positions out here in the open in front of the spectators."

Cries of "St. Bernard" arose from all over the audience.

Mudd, a German Shorthaired Pointer, led the pack with chants of: "We want St. Bernard! We want St. Bernard!"

At all the calls, St. Bernard rose from his seat with his dignified air and bowed low to all the assembled Lucky Dogs.

"Thank you, kind friends," he said, "for your favor, but I wish to introduce a newcomer who will, I hope, take my place tonight as King and Leader of the March. He has just entered heaven and is a Lucky Dog to be proud of. May I present Dukey Daddles! Dukey is a very unusual member of our company, for although he is not yet six months old, he has the poise and size of an Airedale much older. I suggest that Dukey Daddles be chosen King of the Evening."

A bit embarrassed by the praise of his popular friend, Dukey rose and bowed to the audience who was delighted with his appearance.

Shouts of, "He suits us! Welcome, Dukey Daddles!" rang out from every throat until the rows of seats trembled.

The entire crowd agreed at once, and so with cries of "Speech, Dukey! Speech!" four of the larger dogs in the audience rushed upon Dukey and carried him triumphantly on their shoulders to the stage in front of the seats.

There Dukey, in a few well-chosen words, thanked the assembly for their warm welcome and for bestowing on him the extreme honor of being the evening's King and Leader of the March. Then the huge Belgian Sheepdog set upon his head a crown of white ivory with rubies at each point. The whole crowd stood with one accord and cheered till the heaven rang.

To a stirring march from the orchestra, Dukey chose Pfeffer for his partner, and the Grand March began.

Ruth Ann with Whistle Stick and Lonesome with St. Bernard formed the next two couples and were about to fall in line, when a chance glance by Ruth Ann at the Blowster's scale about her neck froze the blood in her veins!

"Goodness me!" she exclaimed to Whistle Stick in a tense whisper. "Look! The scale! It's turned a darker green!"

She showed the scale to Lonesome and the three of them became desperately worried.

"Oh, Dukey," cried the little girl, "you'll excuse us won't you, you and St. Bernard and Pfeffer, if we do not stay with you any longer? We've had such a good time, but the Blowster's scale is turning very dark and we must go! We may be too late already!"

"Why, of course we'll excuse you," answered St. Bernard cordially. "We are sorry that you must go, but we have been delighted to have had you with us even for so short a time as this!"

"Dukey," said Ruth Ann leaning down to give him one last hug, "it almost breaks my heart to leave you, but now I have seen for myself that you'll be well cared for here in the Heaven of Lucky Dogs. Though I will miss you, I am not so sad as before because I know that you will be perfectly happy here among your new friends."

"I, too, feel that I'm going to be happy," agreed Dukey with a glance at Pfeffer. "And I want you to know that I'm going to send a surprise for you to Earth, to remember me by and to keep you from being so sad and lonely."

"Dukey Daddles," pleaded Ruth Ann, "what will it be?"

"That would be telling and spoil the surprise," replied the dog. "But I don't mind telling you that it just may be a birthday present!"

"Come on; let's go," said Whistle Stick gruffly. "We might just as well get that trip to the Blowster's breath over with. I'm not looking forward to it much."

"I'll not mind the ride if we can sail in Flying Fish's passenger basket," responded Lonesome.

"Goodbye then, for the last time, Dukey," called Ruth Ann as she, Whistle Stick, and Lonesome Snake all waved a fond and final farewell to Dukey Daddles and his new friends, the Lucky Dogs. They, in turn, waved back and wished the travelers well.

The trio hastened to the gate, which they found opened easily from the inside. Stooping low, they crept through the gate and fairly flew across the stretch of open country that lay between the Heaven of Lucky Dogs and the place where Official Transport was still waiting patiently.

"Well, well, well," he said drowsily upon seeing his passengers, "are you back already?"

"Already!" panted Ruth Ann. "We've been gone too long, we're afraid! You must have fallen asleep. Mr. Transport, the Blowster's scale is turning black, and we shall have to stay in High Country forever and ever if we can't make it back to his last breath column before he inhales it back to Earth!"

Chapter 22

A Race for Their Lives

 lying Fish seemed to realize the seriousness of the situation at once, for the three friends had scarcely time to seat themselves in the passenger basket when the great transport leaped into the air and began to sail like a bird back in the direction of Pinhead Land.

"How far is it to the entrance of High Country?" he shouted back to them as he flew.

"I haven't the slightest idea," yelled Ruth Ann. "It must be some distance though, because we have to pass over Incorrigible River and Shadow Forest on the way."

"I'll have to stop at the garage, then," Flying Fish cried out. "It's better to take time out right now than to run out of fuel in some out of the way place where there isn't a chance to get any!"

Ruth Ann agreed but grew more and more anxious. She

kept her eyes glued on the Blowster's scale, and it seemed to grow darker every second.

Faster and faster they flew until the air whizzed by them like a cyclone, and she had to keep her hands over her ears to keep out the terrible whirr of it! It was impossible to talk, so she and Whistle Stick and Lonesome Snake huddled together silently in the passenger basket.

After a time that seemed like hours of such travel, they felt the great fish slowing up. Ruth Ann poked her head over the basket edge and saw that the Official Transport was settling down at his own garage for refueling.

"First stop!" he called back cheerfully to his passengers.

"Well, I hope it's the first and last stop," grumbled Whistle Stick. "The mere thought of our being left to spend the rest of our lives in this country makes me stiff all over."

Lonesome Snake did not reply. He had been looking very sad ever since they started. Ruth Ann motioned to Whistle Stick to please be still, as she was afraid that the parting with them was beginning to bear heavily on Lonesome's mind.

Flying Fish did hurry. He floated easily to rest before his garage door, undid his passenger basket, was in and out of his building and tanked up with a new load of fuel in less time that it takes to tell it. He then quickly strapped on the basket again, over his back and under his fins, and was off with a high jump, sailing easily over The Commons and Pinhead Village.

The lights of the town were out and the three watching from the passenger basket could only guess at the location of the little houses.

Ruth Ann couldn't resist a last goodbye to Singing Lantern. So even in the face of the wind that was rushing past her with greater and greater speed, she lifted her head out of the basket and waved her hand at the spot where she imagined the castle.

"Farewell, Your Majesty," she called back softly.

When she sank down again beside her two friends, Ruth Ann could tell that something was amiss. Whistle Stick was gazing moodily ahead of him with an unseeing expression in his eyes, and Lonesome was weeping violently into his red bandana.

"Lonesome," she cried, throwing one arm about poor Lonesome's shoulders, "whatever is the matter?"

"He's a driveling idiot!" remarked Whistle Stick, almost screaming to raise his voice over the force of the wind's roar. In spite of the cruel words, Ruth Ann caught a tremor in his voice that was not put there by his attempt at loud speaking.

"I just can't bear to have you leave me," sobbed Lonesome, heartbrokenly.

"Why, Lonesome, if you don't want to part with us, wouldn't it be possible for you to come back with us? The Blowster's breath will hold up one more I'm sure, and you're not heavy."

Lonesome just shook his head sadly.

"You don't understand, I guess," he replied mournfully. "I can't go back. You can because you chose to be blown up here on the Blowster's breath, but I didn't choose. The mule kicked me up here against my will and so I'll have to stay—and be lonely all my days." He finished with a choking sob.

"Don't cry like that! I can't bear it!" Ruth Ann pleaded. "Isn't there any place in this country where you feel at home?"

At the question, Lonesome brightened up a trifle.

"Yes, there is," he admitted after a moment, "but I don't know how in the world to get there . . . I felt quite at home in Shadow Forest."

"Why, we fly over Shadow Forest on our way to the Blowster's breath!" exclaimed Ruth Ann. Again daring the rushing air, she stood up in the basket and, making a cup of her hands, called out to Flying Fish. They were flying at such speed that it was only with the utmost difficulty that she succeeded in making her voice carry. Even then, Official Transport could not make out her words. He knew that she was trying to reach him with some important message, so he slowed his flight until he could hear her.

"Flying Fish," she shouted, "do you know where Shadow Forest is?"

"Yes," he yelled back. "I've been there with parties of Pin-head sightseers and a few times on my own account. It's a bit out of the way though. Do you want to take time to go?"

Ruth Ann gave a quick glance at the Blowster's scale. It had turned to a still darker green, but being a loyal friend, she called out, "Yes, we'll have to try it, anyway. Lonesome wants to get out there to make a new home for himself."

"All right," answered Flying Fish, "I'll try to make up the time it will take!" Again the Official Transport surged ahead with a whirl and a swirl of wind.

A faint glow was just beginning to cover High Country when the passengers felt Flying Fish slow his great speed.

"I believe I've sighted Shadow Forest below," he shouted back to the others. "Hold everything! I'm slowing up for the drop!"

Half floating, half flying, the great fish came to a full stop on the far side of the forest, almost exactly at the spot where Ruth Ann, Whistle Stick, and Lonesome had entered its vast shades.

It was a lovely time to enter the forest, for the birds were just awakening and the shadow trees were full of chirpings and twitterings. Evidently, the winged occupants had heard the noise of O.T.'s great wings, for the three friends scarcely had time to creep out of the basket when a flock of birds, led by Wingus, flew to greet them.

All the birds except Wingus seemed to hold back somewhat when they saw Lonesome Snake among the newcomers. Wingus, however, was plainly glad to see them all and advanced to the group with a smile.

"Greetings, friends," he said, once again with his dignified air.

"Hello!" replied the visitors all together.

"We are very happy to see you again," went on the bird leader with a little bow. "Won't you come into our forest and make yourselves at home?"

"Thank you," replied Ruth Ann. "But we're in a frightful hurry. We only dropped in to leave Lonesome. This is the only place he's seen since coming to this country that satisfies him. You'll be kind to him, won't you?"

At her words, a smile of delight shone across Wingus's face.

"That's the best message we've had for many a long time!" he cried. "We've often spoken about how lonely the forest seemed without a snake." Here Wingus turned and addressed himself directly to Lonesome Snake. "If you will do us the honor to live here, I know that the other birds and I will consider it a very great honor. A forest without a snake is hardly a forest!"

Lonesome grew positively radiant.

"Here at last, I feel comfortable!" he explained to Ruth Ann. "I can be happy now that I am wanted and accepted as an inhabitant of Shadow Forest. I shall think of you often and if ever you come again . . ."

"We shall think of you often, too, Whistle Stick and I," replied Ruth Ann, "and we shall certainly call on you if we ever visit High Country again."

Whistle Stick could not trust himself to speak, for in his own gruff way, he had grown wonderfully fond of Lonesome. The stick man shook hands as best he could with the snake and quickly turned away, so that the others would not see how the parting moved him.

"We're sorry that we can't stay and visit longer with you," Ruth Ann told Wingus, "but if we don't make the last of the Blowster's breaths, we'll have to stay here forever and ever!"

"Well, if you do miss the breath," returned Wingus, remembering the debt of gratitude he owed the little girl, "you and your friend could just come back *here*—where you would be very welcome in Shadow Forest, I'm sure."

"Whistle Stick and I thank you for your very kind and generous offer and will always remember you and our time here. Now we really must be on our way. Thank you for all you have done for us and Lonesome."

With a sorrowful smile and a wave of her hand, she gently reached for Whistle Stick, encouraging him on and reminding him they had not a moment to spare if they were ever to return home.

The two quickly climbed into Flying Fish's passenger

basket and reminded the Official Transport of the urgency of their flight. They soon found themselves high above Shadow Forest looking down for one last glimpse of Lonesome Snake. Ruth Ann could not be sure but she thought she saw her friend dab at his eyes with his prized red bandana handkerchief. And though she and Whistle Stick would miss him greatly, they knew Lonesome would be happy there with his new friends and that he would no longer be lonely!

On and on the Official Transport flew, desperately trying to make up for lost time, flying farther and farther away from Snake and his new home. Finally, way below, Ruth Ann saw a glint of the little brass door! Almost at that same instant, she looked at the Blowster's scale and her heart leaped into her throat!

"Look, Whistle Stick!" she cried. "The Blowster's scale is turning black!" And sure enough, even as they watched it wide-eyed, the scale turned from the darkest green to jet black!

Frantically, Ruth Ann called out to the Flying Fish!

"We must stop!" she pleaded. "There's the entrance into High Country right below us! I'm afraid we're too late!"

Through the rushing, pushing air, the Fish must have heard the near panic in her call, for without even slowing down, he made a masterful swoop and landed his passengers safely at one side of the little hinged door!

"Thanks a thousand thanks for your kindness and speed, Flying Fish," said Ruth Ann breathlessly. "I do hope we're on time!"

Dragging Whistle Stick by the hand, she rushed him to the door and lifted it on its hinges.

"We're too late," Whistle Stick exclaimed despairingly, "There goes the Blowster's breath . . . look!" And sure enough, a short distance below them the breath column was whirling downward!

"Let's jump!" cried Ruth Ann. "It's the only way! Quick! I'll jump first and you jump right after me. We can't do any more than land in the Highest Country. We'll have to take the risk!"

So saying, she leaped over the edge and felt herself falling down, down, down, until at last, with a gentle thump, she landed safely in the soft, still center of the breath column that gathered about her and held her up like a billowy feather pillow. But what was her horror as she glanced overhead to see far, far above her now, the little face of Whistle Stick, peering at her anxiously through the open door!

"Jump!" she screamed at him. "Jump! Another moment and you will be too late!"

Ruth Ann closed her eyes, for just then she saw Whistle Stick lean far out through the opening and let himself drop clumsily. "He'll never make it!" she moaned to herself. "He waited too long!"

At that very instant she felt something hit her. When she opened her eyes there sat Whistle Stick, right on her chest. She was so glad to see him that she squeezed him with all her might. He pretended that he had known all the time that he was in no danger, and that he could jump down safely beside her.

So reunited, the two friends sat waiting eagerly as the Blowster's column whirled them back again to Earth.

Chapter 23

The Green Blowster, Again

"**L**and sakes!" boomed the great voice of the Green Blowster. "That was a narrow escape for you folks!"

Ruth Ann and Whistle Stick had suddenly found themselves sprawling over a great lily pad in the pool in front of the monster. As they had been swept to Earth on the breath column, they had felt the Blowster's breath suddenly grow warm and dark. The truth of the matter was that the monster had inhaled them into his mouth, and was on the verge of swallowing them entirely when he had felt them against the roof of his mouth. He exhaled them immediately in a great burst of breath.

"That's what happens for being late!" boomed the Blowster. "If I'd ever been late for my breathing practice, you might not be here now! How did you finally get on my breath anyhow?"

"We . . . we jumped!" replied Ruth Ann rather tremblly over their recent experience. "You see we had to stop in Shadow Forest for Lonesome to get out of the Official Transport's passenger basket. That's what made us late. But if you could have seen how happy Lonesome was when we left him, you'd forgive us."

"Humph!" thundered the creature. "Maybe. Maybe. But it certainly was a good thing for you that I felt you against the roof of my mouth just when I did, for if you had been drawn beyond my mouth into my lungs and stomach—I shudder to think . . . " The Blowster paused so the words would have their full effect.

Ruth Ann could not repress a shiver of her own. Quickly her unfailing good spirit returned and she laughed.

"Well, you didn't swallow us, Mr. Blowster," she cried happily, "and here we are at home again. And we've had the most wonderful adventures!"

"You'll have to be mighty quick telling about them!" boomed the creature. "I'm late now in sinking to the depths of the pool."

Without hesitating, Ruth Ann and Whistle Stick took turns giving the Green Blowster a very brief and breathless account of their visit to High Country: of Lonesome Snake and the red bandana, of merry Incorrigible River and his guardian, Loppy Wallops, of the Queen of the Pinheads who sang her "Song of Joy," and of their happy meeting with the Fuzzy-Skinned Grumpus who proved to be none other than Dukey Daddles!

The Green Blowster listened with the keenest interest until they had finished telling their tale.

"A most remarkable night!" he boomed. "I am glad to think that my breathing helped you to enjoy it. However, haven't you forgotten to tell me the most important thing?"

"Why, what?" asked the little girl puzzled.

"Have you forgotten the main reason for my sending you to High Country on my breath column?" thundered the creature.

"No," answered Ruth Ann, although her voice trembled a bit as she remembered back to their conversation with the Blowster earlier that night.

"Well, tell me, then!" the Blowster ordered. "Were there

any in High Country with *lines*? Did you two decide on something that you wanted to do as a reason for living on Earth?"

"We didn't meet any great breathers like yourself up there Mr. Blowster," replied Ruth Ann admiringly. "But we did meet some artists with other *lines*. For instance, there were the Sighing Snails and the Black Weeper, who wept so well that he was hired to do the weeping for a whole country!"

"Humph! They sound interesting. I should like to meet them. But what of you, yourself? Did you decide on a *line*, something that you'd like to practice for?"

"Well," Ruth Ann confessed finally. "I believe that I'd rather write stories than do anything else in the world. I'd like to write all about my adventures in High Country! I'd like my *line* to be writing."

"That doesn't sound half bad!" approved the Green Blowster. "I guess that I'm perfectly safe letting you practice your *line*. You'll probably amount to something yet. Now how about you?" he went on addressing Whistle Stick. "What are you going to do?"

Stick thought for just a moment in silence.

"You know," he stated at last, "I don't believe that I'll ever be happy as long as I'm walking around. I don't believe that sticks were made to move about like boys and girls. I think I'd like to be a tree! I'm just aching to get my tired feet into the ground and stay put for a while!"

"Whistle Stick, what a splendid idea," exclaimed Ruth Ann. "Then on sunny afternoons I can come out and sit beside you and write and write!"

At this point the two friends were interrupted by the thundering tones of the Blowster.

"Well, I guess you both are pretty well settled in your minds about what you want to do, and I feel safe in leaving you. I've heard my call. I always feel a pulling from the depths when my time on Earth is up for the night. If you ever get a chance to come out late again in the evening, be sure to look me up. It's been a pleasure to aid you in your adventures, I'm sure!"

"Thank you, Green Blowster," cried Ruth Ann and Whistle Stick together. "We'll never forget your kindness. Of that you may be sure!"

Slowly the great monster began to sink. His breaths grew lighter and shorter. The two friends left behind watched him in amazement as his great bulk sank from sight. Finally, there was nothing left above the waters of the pool but two great eyes and the top of his head. Then quite deliberately, one of the huge red eyes winked right at Ruth Ann!

"Goodbye!" she waved. And the next moment the Green Blowster was gone! For just a second, there was a slight rippling on the waters, and then all was still. Not a thing disturbed the surface of the pool. It lay as smooth as Mirror Lake under the moon that was hurrying to bed in the west.

Ruth Ann and Whistle Stick looked at one another in awe. It was such a tremendous happening, the sinking of the Green Blowster! One moment he was with them, immense and friendly, and the next moment he was gone, not a sight nor a sound of him anywhere!

That last wink had reassured Ruth Ann that his sinking wasn't as remarkable an occurrence to the Green Blowster himself as it was to them. He had done it many times before and would do it many times again. It was all in his night's work!

"I guess we had better get home now as fast as we can," Ruth Ann remarked, regretfully. "It's been a wonderful night, but even the most wonderful of nights must come to an end."

"Home sounds good to me," agreed Whistle Stick, with a bit of wistfulness in his gruff little voice. "I'm thinking of having a home too, for the first time in my life. Ruth Ann, will you plant me?"

"Plant you?" echoed the little girl.

"Yes! You *will* plant me, won't you?" he begged. "Then I'll stay put and there'll be no more Incorrigible Rivers or terrible Pinheads to vex me. I tell you, sticks are made to grow into trees and not to go traveling around in faraway places on two feet like human beings!"

"Very well, Whistle Stick," agreed Ruth Ann. "If that is the way you will be happiest, I shall be very glad to plant you.

Where do you want to grow?"

"I think I shall feel most comfortable beside Giant's Cap and the Maples," replied Whistle Stick. "I'd like to have you put me there."

Following the directions of the Green Blowster for walking across the water, the two friends skimmed the surface of the pool and then hurried across the stretch of country to Giant's Cap, with the moon falling slowly to sleep. When they reached the cap and the Maples in which Ruth Ann had first sighted the growing grease, they stopped and began to shovel a hole for Whistle Stick in the soft earth with their hands. At last it was ready, and the Stick stepped into his new home with a contented smile on his face.

Ruth Ann shoveled the earth back around his feet with her hands and then shook him just a wee bit to see that he was firmly planted.

"How do you feel?" she asked him a bit anxiously. "Do you feel solid enough so that the first little breeze won't blow you over?"

"Indeed I do!" replied Whistle Stick, in quite a merry voice for him. "My feet are already beginning to take root . . . I do believe. That's the great thing about being a tree. Now you, for instance, grow only at the top, but I'll soon be growing as much under ground as I am above ground!"

"That's so," agreed Ruth Ann. "I'd never thought of that before!"

As she spoke, a sudden darkness crept over the Earth. Ruth Ann realized with a start that the moon had completely disappeared beneath the western horizon!

"Oh, I'll have to be going, Whistle Stick," she said. "I've never been up so late in all my life! I do hope that I get home and in bed before Mother and Father are worried over missing me. I'll see you in the morning."

"Goodnight to you," returned Whistle Stick, a contented smile shining on his face. "I'll rest easy tonight for the first time since I was a little boy's whistle."

"Oh, I'm so glad. It seems as if we've all ended up the night so happily!"

With that, Ruth Ann left her beloved wooden friend and ran joyfully through the deep shadows toward the house that sat like a big white elephant on the crest of the hill. The great trees and their mysterious shadows were no longer frightening to the little girl. She had been, after all, through Shadow Forest in High Country, and Earth trees would never scare her again! She made her way in and out among the oaks and maples to the open field. Then a hop, skip, and a jump across the meadow, and she was climbing the lawn to her front porch. She opened the front door very quietly and crept up the stairs and through the hall to her own bedroom.

When at last, Ruth Ann slipped in between the fresh clean sheets and snuggled her head into her soft comfy pillow, she realized that the adventures of the night had left her very, very weary. She fell asleep almost instantly with a sigh of contentment and a prayer of thankfulness upon her lips. There was so much everywhere for which to be happy!

Chapter 24

Happy Birthday

appy birthday!"

Ruth Ann awoke with a start to find two loving faces bending over her bed. The sun was up and streaming through the windows of her bedroom in great golden rays. What a beautiful day!

"Happy birthday, Ruth Ann!"

Father and Mother were there with the most delightful looking bundles in their arms! Ruth Ann hopped right out of bed and hugged them both in utter happiness.

"Wash and dress as quickly as you can, dear," said Mother. "Father and I will wait right here with your gifts."

"Hold on a minute," added Father as Ruth Ann started to rush into the bathroom. "You can't get away from me until I've given you your birthday pats to remember me by," Father counted as he lovingly patted his daughter, "and one big hug to grow on!"

"Bless me how the child seems to have grown over-
night!" he exclaimed looking up at Mother. They both smiled
proudly and agreed that Ruth Ann was getting to be quite a
young lady.

Never did Ruth Ann get into her rompers more quickly
than she did on this beautiful morning! She was all eagerness
to open those wondrous packages bound in tissue paper and
silk ribbon. She found her socks easily enough—but where
ever were her shoes?

"Mother . . . " she began—then suddenly she remembered!
Her play shoes were sitting, side by side, down near the pool
where she had taken them off so as not to get them muddy in
the wet ground of Cattle Swamp!

"Did you call me, dear?" came Mother's sweet voice.

Ruth Ann, with her magical adventures in High Country
just bursting to be told, managed to keep silent. Grown-ups
were fine and all, and she adored Father and Mother, but she
had a conviction that they would not believe that she had been
blown to High Country. They would probably not even believe
in the Green Blowster! And if they should smile and tell her
that it was all a dream— well, Ruth Ann could not stand even
the thought of that. If they laughed about Whistle Stick and the
Blowster, her birthday would be overshadowed with sadness,
and so she just shut her lips as tight as she could until her
mother called again:

"Didn't you ask me something, dear?"

Finally, Ruth Ann replied, "Never mind, Mother, it wasn't important."

Mother was satisfied and kept talking with Father until Ruth Ann, in her Sunday shoes, appeared in the door of the bedroom and raced across the room and into the arms of both parents for hugs and kisses and birthday gifts!

Never had Ruth Ann been given such lovely presents! There was a new frilly organdy dress from her grandmother in the South, a pearl necklace and bracelet to match from her cousins, a doll from Aunt Caroline with eyelashes of real hair, and a dollhouse that Uncle Bert had made for her. It had a bathroom in it with the 'darlingest' bathtub, just like a grown-up house. There was a box of chocolates and a silk handkerchief with tatted lace around it, and then from Father and Mother, a gold wrist watch with one blood-red ruby set in the center of the back!

Ruth Ann was too happy to speak. She just hugged and kissed her parents, all over again.

Suddenly, she thought of Whistle Stick.

"I'll have to show him my presents," she thought to herself.

"Do you suppose that I could take a short walk before breakfast?" she asked.

"Why, of course dear," answered Mother, "but why?"

"I'm just too happy to stay still," she responded, "and besides, I've got some important things to think over."

Mother said she understood and hugged her daughter very close and kissed her on the forehead. For a moment Ruth Ann thought that Mother really might understand—but still, she kept her secret.

"Run along then, dear! I'll call you when your birthday breakfast is ready."

Mother left the room as Ruth Ann put some of her gifts into her romper pockets. Then, carrying the new doll and the little house, the birthday girl skipped across the hall and down the steps to the field and Giant's Cap.

Her heart leaped when she stopped in front of Whistle Stick and saw the happy light shining in his eyes! Already his arms were as upright as limbs and it even looked as if they were beginning to sprout. Ruth Ann sank with a glad heart to the ground at his feet.

"It's such a comfort to have you to talk to," she sighed, "and this is one of the happiest birthdays I've ever had. What a very lucky girl I am," she continued as she and her friend admired her presents.

"Do you know, Whistle Stick, when I awoke this morning, I almost believed that those wonderful, exciting adventures of last night were really just a dream! Then when I couldn't find my shoes, I knew that they had all been true and that the Green

Blowster really had blown us to High Country on his breath column!"

"Have you been down to the pool to see if your shoes are still there?" inquired the little fellow.

"No, I haven't, but I'm going this minute! Watch my things, please." And with that Ruth Ann was off toward Cattle Swamp, straight as an arrow.

A moment later she reappeared at the side of her friend in triumph, waving two muddy shoes above her head.

"Whistle Stick," she cried, "they were right there, where we put them at the edge of the swamp! It's proof! It all really happened, every bit of it! Why, even Mother and Father would have to believe it!"

"But you're not thinking of telling them, are you?" asked Whistle Stick with a trace of anxiety in his voice.

"Would you," queried Ruth Ann, "if you were in my place?"

"I hardly believe that I would," Whistle Stick answered, after pondering the matter for a moment. "It isn't that we're trying to keep anything from your mother and father you understand. It's just that we want to protect our friend, the Green Blowster. You see, your parents might make it very uncomfortable for him if they found out that he had blown us to High Country—and so late at night. They might even make it impossible for him to enjoy his few hours above water."

"Besides," continued Ruth Ann as she suddenly got another thought, "you remember that I'm going to be a writer. I can write it all out as it really happened and then Mother and Father and everybody can believe it or not, just as they like!"

"That's a grand idea, to my way of thinking," agreed Whistle Stick.

"Ruth Ann, Ruth Ann," Mother's voice came from off in the distance. She was calling, but there was something in her tone of voice that suggested more than the readiness of breakfast.

Ruth Ann waited only long enough to give Whistle Stick a hug and then gathered her parcels and ran back to her home on the hill.

When she got to the porch, there stood her parents looking down at something on the floor at their feet. It was a tiny black and tan ball of fuzz that was trying to stand up on wobbly legs that its fat little belly almost hid!

One look was enough for Ruth Ann!

Down went the beautiful new doll and the little playhouse, and up into her arms she caught the tiny ball of black and tan fuzz and held it tight!

"I can't blame you one bit, Ruth Ann," Father said. "It's the cutest mite of a dog that ever lived, I do believe! Where on Earth did it come from?"

"It's marked just exactly like Dukey Daddles," Mother

added. "That's the peculiar thing. Who do you suppose could have sent it?"

Looking closely at the tiny ball of fluff, Ruth Ann saw that around the puppy's fuzzy neck, tied in a bow over one

of its perky ears, was ribbon of bright green calico. Under the puppy's chubby chin dangled an ornament that looked like the tiny lights on Earth Christmas trees, only this one was shaped like a wee silver bell.

Mother and Father looked very puzzled, but Ruth Ann just smiled, for she knew exactly where it had come from, and who had sent it. Wasn't this adorable puppy marked exactly like him! Mother had even said so.

Ruth Ann could keep her secret no longer.

"Oh," she breathed, "It's from Dukey Daddles! It is! It is!"

"What are you talking about, child?" exclaimed Mother and Father in voices that sounded as one.

"Dukey Daddles sent this surprise to me from High Country, just like he said he would!" she tried to explain.

Mother looked at Father and Father looked at Mother. Then smiling at one another as if to say, "Children certainly do get peculiar notions from time to time," they each gave their daughter a special, tender hug and turned to go in for breakfast.

Following close behind with the new fuzzy puppy held tightly to her heart, Ruth Ann looked at her parents with a smile that came from deep inside and whispered to herself, "Thank you, Dukey Daddles; this is the *best* birthday ever!"